I0822702

Post Apocalypse

A Novel

CONNER ADDICOTT

Post Apocalypse

A Romantic Apocalypse Novel

CONNER ADDICOTT

First Published in 2015 by Addicott Press

Edition 3: This is the hardcover edition.

ISBN: 978-0-9949344-2-0

This is a work of fiction; all characters are based on the authors' imagination. Any likeness to real persons or events is purely coincidental.

This is Book One of the Romantic Apocalypse Series.

CHAPTER 1

In a world where you couldn't be sure of anything anymore, today I was certain of one thing. I would die, I just didn't know how yet. I would've been scared or at least depressed, but I was too weak to really care. In a way I was looking forward to the end and for this constant nightmare to finally be over. I felt like I should've died like all the other people. The fact that I had cheated death somehow and that now this was my punishment, my hell.

The odds were definitely against me and it seemed ironic that I didn't stay alive because I was the fittest or the smartest, but because I was the most scared. When people started to turn into monsters and to kill those who didn't I knew I had to get away from any kind of civilization as far as possible, so I packed my things, got in my car and fled deep into the woods.

I learned the hard way what I could and what I couldn't eat in the wild and spent most of my time in trees. I had tied a long rope to a fire iron, which allowed me to climb even the taller ones, something I came to regret when I fell out of one two months ago and broke my leg. I didn't know how to properly treat an injury like that, so it didn't heal right and now I was walking with a limp. I thought it would be the end of me, because I couldn't run anymore and I was too scared to fight the monsters, but I still didn't die, more out of luck than anything else really.

Then winter hit. When I now imagine hell I don't picture fire and brimstone anymore, I picture the freezing cold of winter and a forest where snow was viciously hiding the very few things left to eat.

I had run out of food days ago and I had a fever. There was a small town a few miles from where I was and it was my only chance to find supplies, but for me to go there was almost certain suicide, because a populated area meant lots of monsters. I didn't even know if I could make it there in my condition, but I was starving and freezing to death, so even the faintest possibility of food and shelter was so overwhelmingly appealing that I decided it was worth dying for.

I opened my toiletry bag and took out my mirror. I barely recognized myself. I was pale and even though I was only eighteen, maybe nineteen, I didn't really look youthful anymore. I had bags under my blue eyes and it showed that I was malnourished. My blonde, slightly wavy hair was greasy and covered more than half of my forehead by now. There was also stubble growing all over the place, so I quickly shaved and then stuffed everything back.

I climbed down my tree and headed to the town. I had to stop several times on the way, but I finally got there after a couple of hours. I hurried from cover to cover, looking out for monsters, till I saw a convenience store up ahead. I crossed the street and silently approached the building. Suddenly a monster came out of an alley behind me. It must have seen me when I walked by. Its eyes were completely black and its skin was very light and looked like paper mâché. Its flesh was dried up and you could see every bone of its skull. I called them monsters, because I was so scared of them, but they were basically zombies. It started to come after me, groaning aggressively. Its movements were very stiff and looked almost mechanical, not human at all anymore. I tried to limp away as fast as I could, but I knew it would catch me within seconds. My eyes were glued to it the whole time, so I didn't see what was in front of me and ran head first into a pole. I fell to the ground and passed out.

The next thing I knew I woke up on the dirty and cold floor of a dim room. The air was moist and stuffy and it felt a little claustrophobic being indoors again after living outside for so long. There was a tall guy sitting on a plastic container across from me, holding a big knife in his hand. He had greasy, dark brown hair that was about as long as mine. His eyes were hazel and he had a very grim looking face, which was covered with a thick beard. He was wearing a long winter coat which had blood splatters all over it and I could smell him from five feet away.

"What happened?" I moaned and propped myself up on my elbow.

"I saved your stupid ass, that's what happened! Now shut the fuck up and take off all your clothes!" he barked at me.

"What? No!"

"Do it right fucking now or I'll stab you in the face!" I started to cry. "Why the fuck are you crying?!" he asked angrily.

"Please don't rape me, please," I whimpered and he frowned deeply.

"Rape you?! Jesus! I wasn't planning to... But if you don't get naked in the next ten seconds I will fucking rape you! Understood?!"

"Yes," I whispered shakily. I quickly got up and undressed completely. I had never been this humiliated in my whole life and I desperately covered my genitals with my hands.

"Lift your arms, spread your legs and then turn around!" he demanded and I obeyed. "Good, now get dressed, quickly!" he said and I put my clothes back on as fast as I could. I was shaking violently from the cold and the fear. He took off his coat and handed it to me. I gratefully wrapped it around my body. It was incredibly warm. "Run off with that and I'll stab you in the face when I catch you! You got that?!" he said warningly.

"Yes, no, thank you."

"Come on, we need to get a fire going."

We started to walk down a long hallway, but I couldn't keep up with him.

"Fucking move it, will ya?!" he barked.

"I'm sorry, this is as fast as I can go."

"Jesus Christ, how the fuck have you survived this long?!"

"I don't know," I mumbled.

We made our way upstairs to what looked like an old storage room. There were a couple of pieces of furniture in one corner and some boxes in the other. He took a chair and pulled it apart like it was made out of matchsticks. When he had enough wood he stacked it all up at the opposite side of the large room.

"You can't light a fire in here, you'll burn the place down or at least the smoke will gather and we might suffocate," I said.

"Shut the fuck up!" he barked and shot me a warning look.

"I'm just saying, it's a bad idea."

He got off his knees, drew his knife and glared at me.

"Do you want me to rape you?!" he asked. My eyes widened and I forcefully shook my head. "That's what I thought. Now sit down and only speak when you're spoken to! You got that?!" I nodded and quickly sat down.

He opened two windows on both sides of the room and lit the fire. To my surprise the smoke escaped through the windows and soon the whole pile was burning. I reached out and warmed my hands over the flames. After maybe half an hour of silence only embers were left. He pulled a can of beans out of his backpack and opened it with his knife. He heated them up and then started to eat them. I watched him wide-eyed. When he caught me I quickly looked away. A couple of minutes later he suddenly handed me the can. It was still half full.

"Eat!" he barked.

I hastily poured the beans into my mouth and swallowed them without chewing. I was a little out of breath when I had finished the can. I took my finger and cleaned out every last drop. Suddenly I felt nauseated and threw up. I sadly stared at the small pile of vomit on the floor, completely disheartened.

"Jesus! How fucking stupid are you?!" he said angrily and slapped me on the back of my head. It didn't hurt that much, but it startled me and I flinched. "That was my last can you fucking retard!" he added.

"I'm sorry," I said shakily.

"Yeah, you will be if I don't find more food soon."

He pulled out a bottle of water and handed it to me. I took a big gulp and immediately had to cough and gag.

"Jesus, do I have to kick your ass?! Take it easy, for fuck's sake!"

"Sorry," I replied and took a smaller sip, but had to cough again. I covered my mouth and looked at him wide-eyed.

"That cough sounds rough. You're not sick or something, are you?" he asked. I slowly nodded and he touched my forehead, which made me flinch again. "God damn it, you're burning up!... Now I can't drink out of that bottle anymore!... Fuck!... I should fucking kill you!" I started to cry and hugged my legs to my chest. My whole body was shaking violently. "Stop crying right now!" he demanded angrily, but that only made it worse. "Jesus fuck!" he cursed, got up and walked away.

By the time he was back, maybe an hour later, the fire had completely gone out, because I had felt too weak and shaken to get up and add more wood, but I had at least stopped crying. He was carrying a steel bucket and what looked like torn up drapes.

"Do you have something to sleep in?" he asked.

"Yes, a plastic tarp."

"That's it?"

"Yes?" I answered nervously.

"No wonder you're sick. Here, you can use this for tonight," he said and handed me his sleeping bag. I rolled it out and slipped inside. It reeked, but it was really warm.

He soaked a piece of cloth in the bucket and offered it to me. "Put this on your forehead," he said and I did. The cold felt very pleasant against my hot skin. "And drink the water, it's yours now anyway," he added and I nodded.

He broke more furniture and restarted the fire. I hadn't been this comfortable in a long time. He sat down next to me and sucked on his finger. He kept doing that and occasionally looked at it, frowning. I raised my right hand, like in school.

"What is it?" he asked sharply.

"Do you have a splinter in your finger?"

"Yes, so?"

I opened my backpack, took the tweezers out of my toiletry bag, got up and kneeled down in front of him.

"Give me your hand please," I said and he reluctantly did. It was pretty big and felt rough. It had calluses all over and his nails were too long and really dirty. There were three splinters in his finger, so I carefully pulled them out one by one. I had to think of the mouse getting the thorn out of the lion's paw.

"Why the fuck do you have tweezers?" he asked, annoyed and frowning, when I let go of his hand.

"I don't know," I said sheepishly.

"And you don't have a beard. Don't tell me you carry around a whole toiletry bag."

"Yeah, so?"

"Jesus Christ, are you actually retarded?"

"No and it's not that stupid, I mean, you'd still have splinters in your finger if I hadn't kept the tweezers, now wouldn't you?" His eyes filled with rage. He grabbed me by the throat and drew his knife.

"Next time you talk back to me it'll be the last thing you'll ever say! You got that?!" I nodded, terrified, and a tear ran down my face. He let go of me and I quickly climbed back into the sleeping bag. I pulled it over my head and cried myself to sleep.

When I woke up it was morning and I could hear the fire crackle. I peeked out and saw him sitting next to me. I watched the fire for a while, but then nature called, so I opened the sleeping bag, sat up and raised my hand. He shook his head and sighed.

"You can talk, just don't say anything stupid or disrespectful," he said.

"Ok, thank you... I need to pee. Where can I go?"

"I'll come with you." I nodded and we got up. After walking a few steps I suddenly felt really weak and collapsed. He caught me and helped me to steady myself.

"When was the last time you ate?" he asked.

"A couple of days ago." I said.

"I see. Come here."

He picked me up and carried me downstairs. I relieved myself in a corner of a small and really horrible-smelling room and then he carried me back.

"Give me my coat," he said and I handed it to him. He opened his backpack and pulled out a can of corn.

"I thought you didn't have any more food."

"This is not for us. I need it to catch a deer," he answered.

"How? Deer don't eat corn."

"I saw a deer eat garbage once, so they'll love this. I'll just have to wait in some bushes long enough and then blast it with my shotgun."

"If you say so."

I though his plan was ridiculous, but I didn't dare tell him.

"I'll barricade the entrance downstairs, so you should be safe, but you do have a weapon, just in case, right?" he said.

"Not really, no."

He looked at me like I was crazy.

"How do you kill the freaks then?"

"I've never killed anyone or anything in my life."

"How is that even possible? You had to get attacked at some point."

"No, I stayed in trees most of the time."

"That's so fucking stupid."

"No, it was actually pretty smart." My eyes widened. "I'm so sorry, I mean, you're right, it was stupid," I said, panicked.

"You starved half to death, got really sick and you probably broke your leg jumping or falling out of a fucking tree. Tell me how that's smart?"

"No, it wasn't, it was really stupid."

"That's right... Here, take my gun," he said and handed me a small revolver. "Do you know how to use that?"

"No?"

"You take the safety off and pull the trigger, very easy. Always aim at their heads or they won't die. Got it?"

"Yes."

"I'll be back before night fall. Keep the fire going, alright?"

"Ok." I said. He nodded and left.

I spent the next couple of hours dozing in the sleeping bag, enjoying the warmth, fantasizing about a hot meal and every once in a while putting more wood on the fire. Suddenly I heard a gunshot in the distance, but maybe thirty minutes later he still wasn't back, so I started to worry and went to the window. I didn't see him and then there was noise coming from downstairs. I quickly pulled out the gun and held it up shakily. After a few moments he appeared and I sighed in relief. He was carrying something on his back and when he dropped it on the floor by the fire, I realized what it was.

"You killed a fawn?" I asked, incredulous.

"Yeah, you got a problem with that?" he said warningly.

"No," I answered meekly.

He started to skin and gut the poor animal. It was disgusting. When he was done he cut off a small piece, stuck it on his knife and held it over the fire. After ten minutes or so he offered it to me.

"No, thank you," I said.

"Are you shitting me right now?!" he barked angrily.

"No, I'm not going to eat a fawn and you can't make me."

He shot up, grabbed me by the jaw and forced open my mouth, shoved in the meat, and covered half my face with his hand so I couldn't breathe.

"Eat it or die!" he barked angrily. I quickly chewed and swallow it. He let go of me and I gasped for air. He sat back down and cut off another piece of meat. I started to cry silently. When I sniffled he looked over and frowned deeply.

"Why are you crying?" he asked, but I didn't answer. "I had to do that. In case you're too stupid to realize it, you were about to starve to death, so I've saved your life, again."

"Why do you even care?" I asked.

"Cause you're with me now, so I have to keep you alive."

"I'm not 'with you' and I don't want to be."

"Well, you can't leave, you'd die for sure."

"So I'm your prisoner now?"

"You know what, you ungrateful little shit, why don't you fucking leave right now? You can even keep my gun."

I thought about it for a second. He seemed like a very unpleasant human being and I had never encountered someone like him before, so I didn't know what to expect. He was really aggressive, abusive even, and I was afraid he still might rape me at some point. But what was the alternative? Starving or freezing to death? Or worse, getting ripped apart by a monster? As much as I hated to admit it, staying with him was my best shot at surviving the winter.

"What's the matter?! Beat it already!" he barked.

"I would like to stay please," I said meekly.

"Oh really? Interesting. So here are the conditions. You will respect me, you will do whatever I tell you, when I tell you, and no more crying. You got that?!"

"Yes."

"Good."

When another piece of meat was ready he offered it to me. I took it without hesitation and put it in my mouth. It wasn't actually that bad.

"Thank you." I said, but he didn't respond. "What's you name? Mine's Cody."

"Troy."

"How old are you? I'm eighteen, maybe nineteen, I'm not sure."

"Twenty-three."

"Have you been alone the whole time since... you know?

"No."

"What happened?"

"What the fuck do you think?" he asked angrily.

"I'm sorry," I said sadly and looked down.

We ate the fawn in silence for the next hour or so. It was nice and warm in front of the fire and I felt a little stronger after every piece of meat Troy gave me.

"I need to get some sleep and you have to keep watch. If you hear anything at all you wake me up immediately. I don't care if it turns out to be nothing, but if I wake up and there are freaks in here or I find you asleep I will pull out all your teeth and use you as a human sex doll. I will also amputate all your limbs one by one and eat them. And when there's only the torso left of you I will let the freaks rip you apart. Am I making myself clear?!" he said. I looked at him wide-eyed and nodded forcefully.

He gave me his coat and climbed into his sleeping bag. The fire went out maybe half an hour later and it became dark. I was pretty tired, but the thought of what he'd do to me if I'd fall asleep kept me wide-awake. I wasn't sure if he was serious or if he was only trying to scare me, but I didn't want to find out.

In the morning Troy started a new fire and we had more fawn for breakfast.

"What are we going to do when we run out of meat?" I asked.

"We? You mean what am I going to do, right?"

"I could help."

"Oh yeah? How exactly?"

"I don't know," I said sheepishly.

"You're good for nothing, but I'll figure something out, don't worry."

"Ok."

After we had eaten Troy disappeared for a couple of hours. I spend most of that time taking little naps and keeping the fire going. He was back in the afternoon, with a large steel barrel. He emptied it on the floor and out came a grillage, a couple of bricks, some electric cords and a lot of twigs and small branches.

"What are you going to do with all that stuff?" I asked curiously.

"Save our asses."

Over the next hour or so I watched how he pulled the wire out of the cords, lit a fire in the barrel and then closed the lid with pieces of meat hanging from it on the wire. I was pretty impressed. I wouldn't have thought of that. He also built a grill over the fire and soon we were eating what was left of the fawn. For the first time in months I was actually full. My fever had gone down too and when I was lying in the warm sleeping bag I felt really good and wasn't even that afraid anymore. It was almost surreal and I was deeply grateful.

"Troy?" I asked quietly.

"What is it?" he replied, annoyed.

"Thank you so much for helping me."

"Whatever."

"Troy?"

"Jesus, what?"

"Oh, nothing, sorry."

"Just fucking ask already."

"Why did you make me get naked?"

"I had to check if you were bitten, didn't I?"

"You could've just asked."

"Right, cause you would've just told me."

"Why would I keep something like that from you?"

"Cause I would've killed you immediately."

"What? Why?"

"For fuck's sake, don't you know anything?"

"Sorry."

"If you get bitten by a freak you turn into one."

"Oh, I didn't know that."

"Now you do."

"Have you killed a lot of them?"

"Yes."

"How many?"

"I don't know, over a hundred probably."

"Have you ever felt bad about it?"

"No and I won't feel bad about killing you either if you don't shut up and go to sleep."

"Sorry. Good night."

I closed my eyes and fell asleep soon after. The next morning I was roughly shaken awake by Troy.

"Get the fuck up, we're leaving!" he barked.

"Where are we going?"

"The next town."

"Ok."

He had already packed everything, so I rolled up the sleeping bag and he tied it to his backpack. We went outside and started to walk down the street. I tried really hard to keep up with him, but couldn't.

"We'll never make it before dark at this pace," he said, frustrated.

"I'm sorry."

He thought for a second and then suddenly looked in my direction with a grim expression, drew his knife and sprinted towards me.

"No! Please don't kill me! You can just leave me! Please!" I said, panicked.

I knew it was pointless to run or to try to defend myself, so when he had almost reached me, I covered my face with my arms and squatted down. I heard a cracking sound and then a thud. I looked behind me and there was a dead monster lying on the ground. Troy cleaned his knife on the corpse, took off his backpack and buckled it on his chest.

"Get on my back, quickly," he said.

"You want to carry me? Are you sure?"

"What the fuck did I say about doing what I fucking tell you?!" he barked.

"Sorry," I said nervously and quickly climbed on his back. He started to walk, pretty fast actually.

After a mile or so a female monster tumbled out of the forest, maybe a hundred yards in front of us. Her clothes were partially torn off and her left breast was exposed, but it was ripped open and all the fat had poured out, so it was flapping around like a bloody rag. It was gross. She saw us and headed in our direction. Troy didn't seem to care.

"You see her, don't you?" I asked.

"Shut the fuck up!" he answered, a little out of breath.

Right before she reached us he drew his knife and then stabbed her in the head violently. She dropped to the ground with a thud and stopped moving.

"Say 'hi' to the devil for me, bitch," he said and cleaned his knife on her clothes.

"Do you like killing them?"

"Sure, why?"

"You haven't killed any normal people yet, have you?"

"No, but keep talking and I will kill you."

"Sorry."

I wasn't sure what I should make of Troy carrying me. It was such a lovely gesture for someone who was so aggressive and who seemed more or less hostile towards me. But in a weird way I kind of enjoyed it. The sun was shining, his body was really warm and whenever I slid down on him too much he adjusted me, so I was always pretty comfortable. The only thing that bothered me a little was that he smelled of old sweat, smoke and curdled blood. After a couple of hours we came across a gas truck at the side of the road.

"Wait here," he said and let me down.

He walked to the door and slowly opened it. Suddenly a monster fell out. He quickly stabbed it in the head before it could get up. He climbed into the truck and searched it for maybe ten minutes. He came out with a map in his hand and studied it for a while.

"Let's go," he said and I got on his back again.

We walked for a long time and he only stopped once for a couple of minutes. I was really impressed by his stamina. I was getting tired just from holding on to him. Of course I kept that to myself. At one point we took a turn, off the concrete road, onto a small path, leading into the woods.

"Where are we going?" I asked, surprised.

"Shut the fuck up!"

"Sorry."

CHAPTER 2

After at least another five miles a house appeared in the distance. We walked up to it and he let me down again. The door seemed untouched, which I took as a good sign that we might find food and other useful things in there. With his knife and a lot of brute force Troy managed to get it open without making too much noise. We entered the house and I pulled out my gun.

"Put that away, I don't wanna get shot by your stupid ass," he said quietly and I obeyed.

Everything looked hauntingly peaceful, like nothing had ever happened. We walked through the living room, which led to a hallway, and the first room on the right was the kitchen. There were two pretty horrible-smelling monsters sitting across from each other on the floor. They slowly tried to get up when they saw us, but Troy quickly stabbed them both in the top of their heads and they lifelessly dropped back down. On the counter there was a holder with kitchen knives. He pulled out the biggest one and handed it to me.

"Into the brain, as hard as you can," he said and I nodded.

We went back to the hallway and checked every room till we came to the stairs leading up. I got startled by a monster that was lying on the landing where the stairs took a turn. It wasn't a regular monster though. It used to be a little boy, maybe ten years old. It seemed like he had broken his neck and couldn't move anymore, but he started to groan and hiss as soon as he saw us. Troy didn't hesitate for a second and brutally stomped on his head, which burst like a watermelon and splattered blood all over the wall and the stairs. I almost gagged, but managed to hold it back. We checked the second floor and then went down to the basement. In one corner we found two shelves with jars and cans of food.

"Jackpot... I guess I won't have to eat you after all," he said and I swallowed hard.

"You're only joking, aren't you?" I asked nervously.

"Shut the fuck up," he answered, frowning.

He searched the whole basement and after a while he held up a camping stove.

"We're gonna take a warm bath tonight," he said almost cheerfully.

"But we don't have any water."

"There's a well out back."

"Oh, ok. And you want to heat up the water with that little thing? That won't work. It'll take way too long."

"No, retard, we'll fill the tub, then put this under it and heat up the whole thing at once."

"That's ridiculous." My eyes widened. "I mean, yeah, that will work," I added quickly and looked at him nervously.

"You know what? No bath for you. And I won't let you get in bed with me filthy like that, so you're gonna sleep on the floor. How do you like that, smart-ass bitch?"

"I'm sorry," I said, defeated.

"That's right. Now let's get a move on, we have a lot of work to do before it gets dark."

"We do?"

"Yeah, well, me mostly. You are in charge of searching every inch of this place for anything that could be useful and then you pack as much of it as we can both possibly carry. Don't pack the stuff in the bathroom though and not all the food. Alright?"

"Why, are we not staying here?"

"We are, for now, but I wanna be ready to bolt at any time."

"Ok."

I thought he was being really paranoid, because the house seemed more or less secure, so I didn't see any reason why we'd have to leave before we'd run out of food. But I didn't want to upset him by arguing, because he didn't seem as hostile as usual and I wanted to keep it that way.

While I was searching the house he was barricading the doors and windows and then started to bring in water from the well two buckets at a time. Last he dragged out the corpses and then blocked the kitchen door as well. I had found very few things that were actually useful, except for a bottle of painkillers. I had immediately taken two pills and after half an hour or so I already felt a little better.

"Did you find any booze?" he asked when everything was done.

"Yes?" I answered nervously.

"Where?"

"Please don't get drunk, ok?"

"Why the hell not?"

"You know, because some people get violent when they are drunk."

"I'll get violent right now if you don't tell me where the fucking booze is."

"In the cabinet behind the couch, in the living room."

"And you didn't think to pack it? Do I have to beat some fucking sense into you?"

"No, I'm so sorry, I wasn't thinking." He just shook his head, frowning, and walked away.

"Hell yeah! Right fucking on!" I heard him yell from the living room.

He came back with a bottle of whiskey in his hand, took two glasses out of a cupboard and filled them.

"Bottoms up," he said and downed his glass. He began pouring a second glass, and filled the second half way. He motioned it towards me.

"No thanks. I don't drink." I said.

"You do now. Let's go." He winked, and forced the glass into my hand. It wasn't sinister, but something tells me the wink was for no good.

I hesitantly picked up the whiskey and carefully took a small sip. I immediately had to cough.

"You're such a fucking pussy. Just down the fucking thing," he said, annoyed, so I did and had to cough again. My throat was burning and my stomach started to feel really warm all of a sudden. It was actually kind of nice.

"There you go," he said and tried to pour me another, but I quickly held my hand over the glass.

"No thanks, I really shouldn't drink, I'm still sick, you know?"

"Fine, whatever, more for me," he answered, frowning, and took a big gulp right out of the bottle.

"Come," he said and I followed him down to the basement.

"What'll it be?" he asked me in front of the shelves with all the food.

"The sardines maybe?"

"No, pick at least three things and a dessert."

"Shouldn't we try to make this last for as long as possible?"

"Fuck that, we could die tomorrow, hell, we could die today, so let's enjoy ourselves while we still can."

"Ok, then the sardines, the green beans and the peas... and peaches for dessert."

"Alright, let's get this stuff upstairs."

I took my cans and he chose corned beef, sausages, mushrooms and pears. We carried them to the kitchen and checked the stove. It was still working. Next we went to the first floor, into the master bedroom. We searched the closet, but everything was a little too big for me.

"Look through the chick's stuff, it might fit you," he said.

"I'm not wearing women's clothes."

"Either that or you'll walk around naked."

I reluctantly looked through the woman's wardrobe and embarrassingly enough I found a pair of sweatpants and a couple of t-shirts that would fit me perfectly. Troy found something too and we went into the bathroom together.

"Check the water," he said and kneeled down to search the cabinet under the sink. I dipped a finger into the water in the tub and to my surprise it was really warm.

"It's ready," I said.

"Good, get in."

"But you said I couldn't take a bath." He just shot me a warning look. "No, yes, thank you... Are you going to give me some privacy maybe, please?"

"Don't be such a coy-ass bitch. Jesus. Now get in before I change my mind."

I turned away from him, quickly took off my clothes and got into the tub. The water felt amazing. I leaned back and slid down till I was covered up to my neck and sighed contentedly. I looked over to Troy, but he was busy cutting his beard with a pair of scissors. For the next ten minutes or so I just enjoyed the warmth. It was the first time I had felt almost relaxed since the world ended.

"Start washing yourself," he said when he was nearly done shaving. He looked really handsome without the beard. His face wasn't as hard-featured as it had seemed before. It was still manly, but a lot friendlier and he had one of those dimples on his chin, which I thought was pretty attractive.

I washed my hair first and then the rest of my body. Troy turned off the camping stove and disappeared with it. When he came back I was just about to get out of the tub, so I quickly covered my genitals. He just raised his eyebrows and shook his head. I climbed out and he undressed and got in. I wanted to look, but I didn't dare. I dried myself off and put on my new clothes.

"Go eat and when you're done start preparing my stuff. I'll be down in fifteen minutes," he said.

"Ok."

I went downstairs and had dinner. It was amazing. I actually licked my plate after I was finished eating. I heated up Troy's food and just when it was about to be ready he walked in. I watched him wolf it down and then we both took our desserts and went back upstairs.

"If you have to piss or shit do it now, cause I'll barricade the door for the night," he said.

"No, I'm good."

When I entered the bedroom I was hit by a wave of warm air and noticed the camping stove on the floor. Had he told me he wanted to heat up the room with it I would've thought it could never work. Maybe I wasn't the smartest after all.

He pushed the wardrobe in front of the door and we got into bed, I on the right, by the window, and he on the other side. We leaned against the headboard and started to eat our dessert. I looked outside. The sun was setting and painted the sky in the most beautiful red and orange colors. For a brief moment I almost forgot everything around me and just felt contented. When I was done eating, I put the empty can on the nightstand and rubbed my stomach. It was really full and was sticking out a little.

"This is nice," I said.

"Yeah, it's just weird that I'm in bed with another dude, but you're more like a little girl, so I guess it doesn't count."

I chose to ignore his rude comment.

"I know, when I pictured myself sharing a bed with another guy I didn't imagine it would be like this either." My eyes widened as soon as the words had left my mouth.

"What? You're a fag?" he asked sharply.

"No?" I answered, panicked. He grabbed me by the throat and drew his knife.

"I'll ask you one more time and you better not be lying, cause that would mean you're disrespecting me and then I'd have to stab you! So, are you a fag or not?!"

I was terrified and I didn't know what to answer. I was sure I'd get stabbed either way.

"Yes," I finally whispered shakily. His eyebrows went up and he let go of me.

"Seriously? You're a full-on fag? For real?"

"Yeah?"

"Well, that's sort of good news actually."

"It is?" I asked, completely dumbstruck.

"I guess. Now lie down on your stomach."

"What? Why?"

"I'm gonna fuck the shit out of you."

"No! You can't do that!... I mean, please don't do that! Please!" I said, horrified.

"Why the hell not? You're a fag, so you like it up the ass, right?"

"No, I don't. Anal sex is very invasive. I've read that it can hurt pretty badly the first time. I'd only let someone do it who I'm in love with. Someone I trust. You know?"

"Are you saying you wouldn't LET me do it?! Do you think you could stop me?!"

I started to cry.

"Please don't, please," I whimpered.

"Jesus, fine, I won't fuck you, but only if you stop crying right now."

I quickly wiped away my tears and tried to pull myself together.

"Thank you," I said shakily.

"Now, a blowjob isn't 'invasive' and doesn't hurt, right? And fags love to suck cock. So go ahead, blow me instead."

"No, please."

"Are you shitting me?! What's your excuse now, you ungrateful little shit?! I've saved your life a couple of times now, so this is the very fucking least you can do for me!" he said angrily.

I thought about it for a second. I had read once that if you're getting raped you should do whatever the rapist says or it would only get worse. And I really didn't have any other option. Maybe it wouldn't be too bad. He was clean and he would probably ejaculate pretty fast.

"Ok, I'll do it," I said, defeated.

"There you go."

He lay back, pulled down his pants and closed his eyes. His penis was still soft, but already kind of big. I reluctantly took it in my hand and leaned down, but I couldn't bring myself to put it in my mouth. I started to cry again and a tear dropped down on his testicles. He opened his eyes and frowned deeply.

"Jesus Christ, what the fuck is wrong with you?!" he barked angrily. I quickly hid under the covers and started to sob. "Stop being such a fucking pussy!"

"Please don't rape me, please." I pleaded through my tears.

"God damn it, you're so fucking sensitive!" he said and pulled off my blanket. I curled up in a ball and started to shake violently.

"Jesus, I'm not gonna rape you! Now stop being so fucking scared!" That calmed me down a little, but I was still very upset. Suddenly I felt his hands on my shoulders, massaging me, but very roughly.

"Oww, you're hurting me!" I cried out.

"Jeeesus fucking Christ, I was just trying to comfort you!" Before I could respond he grabbed me under my arms and pulled me to him till my head was on his lap. I looked at him wide-eyed and he started to scratch my scalp.

"That hurts too," I said and he inhaled sharply.

"Dogs love that."

"Well, I'm not a dog."

"What the fuck do you want me to do then?"

"Just stroke my hair, if you want. But gently."

He tried, but used too much force and pulled my hair with every stroke.

"No, like this," I said, took his hand and guided it softly over my head.

"You're shitting me, right? I'm barely touching you. Can you even feel that?"

"Yeah, I can feel it just fine."

"You're fucking weird."

"No, I'm not. You are." My eyes widened. "No no, you're not weird, at all. I am," I quickly added.

"That's right." He said as he stroked my hair for another ten minutes or so and I calmed down considerably. Then he suddenly realized that he still had a bottle of whiskey waiting for him. He took a big gulp out of it and I tried to get up, but he held me down.

"What's the matter? I thought you liked this," he said.

"I do, but you're getting drunk, so I want to get out of your way."

"Relax, I'm not a mean drunk." He said and winked with a grin.

"I find that hard to believe."

"Cody!" he said warningly. "Jesus, even your name sounds like you're a little boy. From now on your name is Hank, so there's at least one thing manly about you."

"Thanks a lot," I said sarcastically.

"Hey, it's not my fault that you're such a weak, stupid, crippled, pussy-ass bitch."

"So I guess you're done being nice to me?"

"I'm always nice to you."

"That's a joke, right?"

"No, keeping you alive is pretty damn nice, wouldn't you say so?"

"Yes, I'm sorry. You do seem to care about me, in your own way."

"Now let's not go crazy. You're like a pet to me, nothing more."

"Really?" I asked and looked down.

"Shut the fuck up."

I was still a little shaken, but I had been alone for so long that it felt really good being touched by someone in a kind way again. And I appreciated that he was trying to comfort me. It made me wonder if he wasn't such a bad guy after all. I had been sure he would rape me, but he didn't, even though he easily could have, so maybe it was never his intention in the first place. And maybe he didn't want to hurt me either. We didn't talk for a while and he finished the whole bottle of whiskey.

"Christ, if the freaks came a knockin' right now we'd be totally fucked," he said, more to himself than me, and laughed.

"I could fight them off." I said and he laughed harder.

"Sure. By the way, where's your knife?"

"I left it downstairs," I said sheepishly.

"That's probably for the best. You would only cut or stab yourself with it accidentally."

"I'm not that clumsy and my arms are pretty strong, from climbing trees, you know?"

"Right, I almost forgot."

"Why do you call them freaks anyway?"

"Cause they're freaks of nature and everything about them is crazy."

"I think they look like monsters."

"Monsters are something you're scared of. You shouldn't be scared of them, fear only cripples you. And they're stupid and slow, which makes them easy to kill." He laughed. "Like you in a way," he added.

"Why do you always have to put me down?" I said.

"It's called 'tough love' ...Not that I love you. Jesus, I really am drunk."

"Did you mean it when you said I'm no more than a pet to you?"

"Yeah, a really annoying, stupid, crippled pet."

"If I'm so annoying, why do you keep me around? I only slow you down and drain your supplies. So why not cut me loose?"

"Cause you're like a walking, talking emergency ration. When I run out of food someday I can always eat you," he said and laughed. I tried to get up again, but he didn't let me.

"Let go of me, I don't want to be anywhere near you, and tomorrow I'll pack my stuff and leave first thing. I'm not taking your abuse just to end up getting eaten by you."

"Shut the fuck up! You're not going anywhere, you got that?!"

"You can either let me leave or you kill me right now," I said, determined.

"Why do you have to be such a fucking pain in the ass?! I was only kidding, I won't fucking eat you, alright?! Now settle down!"

We looked into each other's eyes for a moment, but I still didn't feel better about the whole thing.

"So why do you keep me around then?"

"None of your fucking business."

"That's not good enough. I can't be scared of you all the time, that's no better than being out there on my own."

"Just shut the fuck up already. You're starting to piss me off."

"So what, you're going to kill me if I don't?" I asked challengingly and tried to push away the hand he was holding me down with. Suddenly he grabbed me by the throat and drew his knife.

"Enough!" he yelled furiously. I had convinced myself that he wouldn't hurt me, but now I felt all the more terrified when I realized what a mistake I had made and in how much trouble I was in for provoking him, so I started to cry. He let go of me and lowered his knife.

"Stop crying!" he yelled. But I couldn't, I just stared at him fearfully.

"Fine, you wanna know why, you little shit? Alright. I keep you alive cause I think you might be an angel."

That really shocked me. On the one hand it was almost kind of sweet, but on the other hand it scared me a little, because I was afraid he might be insane.

"You think I'm an angel?" I asked nervously.

"Well, you look like one, but I'm not crazy, so I think it's unlikely that you're an actual angel from heaven or anything. But you're at least the next best thing. Think about it, you shouldn't have been able to survive on your own for so long, but you did somehow, which is a small miracle in itself if you ask me. What's more amazing though is the fact that you seem untouched by this hellish nightmare we live in. You're still good and innocent, which makes you such a rarity. Something like that has to be protected at all costs and I'd die before I'd let anything happen to you."

I was totally stunned by this. He actually really cared about me.

"If I'm so special, why aren't you treating me better?" I asked cautiously.

"This is a harsh world. I think under the circumstances I've been very soft and patient with you. You're just incredibly sensitive, like a little girl."

"I'm not that sensitive, I just don't want to be 'handled' like I'm your dog or something."

"Are you not safe, clean, full and lying in a warm bed right now? What more do you want? That I sing you a fucking lullaby?"

"That's what I mean, you constantly insult me and you order me around and threaten me. That has to stop."

"It has to? Or what? You'll leave?"

"Yes, I will."

"You know what? Go right ahead, leave. I won't stop you." There was a long pause. "What the fuck are you waiting for?! Get lost!"

"Fine, I won't leave," I said quietly.

"That's what I thought."

"But you have to be nicer to me." I said, and I stared him right in the eyes.

"I have to do shit! But how about I beat you bloody now, gag you and then lock you in the closet for the rest of the night for being disrespectful to me?!" My eyes widened with fear and I teared up again. "For fuck's sake!" he said angrily and quickly stroked my hair. Weirdly enough, it calmed me down a little.

"Why is it so important to you to be respected?" I asked after a few minutes. He was still stroking my hair.

"Cause I've earned it."

"Haven't I earned it too?"

"No, you just climbed on trees like a fucking monkey and hid. I had to fight to survive. You have no idea what I had to go through."

"I see... Why do you hate it so much when I cry?"

"I just do, alright?"

"I'm sorry I cry so much, I guess I am a little too sensitive, but I can't help it, I just get really scared when you're threatening me."

"It's not like I would ever really hurt you or anything."

"You've already hurt me a couple of times now, emotionally, you know? But also physically, when you were too rough with me."

"I didn't mean to do that and I'm not trying to be rough with you, I'm just not used to being careful." He said.

"Maybe I could teach you." I tried to touch his hand, but he pulled his away.

"I'm not gonna become some weak-ass pussy-bitch like you."

"But you could pretend to be, for me? I won't think any less of you. On the contrary, I will admire you even more than I already do."

"You admire me?"

"Of course and I'm deeply grateful for all you've done for me."

"Then fucking act like it."

"I will, I promise."

"Alright, so what do I do differently?"

"You could stop barking orders at me and maybe start saying 'please'."

"That's not gonna happen." He laughed.

"And how about you stop threatening to hurt me, period?"

"Then how do I get you to do stuff?"

"By saying 'please'."

He inhaled sharply. "Whatever." He agreed.

"And you could also stop insulting me all the time, I'd really appreciate that."

"Don't be such a fucking pussy. Jesus." He rolled his eyes and I gave him a more serious look.

"But it bothers me."

"Just shut the fuck up already, alright?! This discussion is over!"

"Fine." I said and scooted back to my side of the bed and covered myself up.

"Now let's get some sleep, I'm fucking beat."

"Good night," I said.

"Yeah, night."

The room turned quiet. I closed my eyes and fell asleep minutes later.

CHAPTER 3

I was woken by a loud groan and then I felt something biting me in the arm. I screamed in terror, jumped backwards and fell to the floor.

"HELP! TROY! HELP!" I yelled, but then I heard hysterical laughter coming from the bed and realized that it was Troy who had bitten me. I got up and glared at him.

"Oh shit, that was priceless," he said, a little out of breath.

"How could you do that do me? I was scared to death," I said indignantly.

"Oh relax, it was just a joke. Don't get your panties all in a bunch."

I pulled up my sleeve and found a bite mark on my arm.

"Look what you've done, I'm bleeding."

"You'll live."

"I think I deserve an apology."

"How about I give you the finger instead and you shut the fuck up already?" he said and flipped me off. I quickly got back into bed, turned away from him and hid under the covers.

"I will stay here till you've apologized," I said.

"Whatever."

I heard him get up, push the wardrobe aside and leave. I stayed in bed all morning. I felt stupid, but I couldn't let him win. Around noon he came back and put something on the nightstand.

"Eat this, you sulky-ass bitch," he demanded. When I didn't react he sighed heavily. "Please?" he said, annoyed.

I lifted the blanket a little and peeked out. There was a steaming bowl with what smelled like tomato soup. I loved tomato soup. I quickly grabbed it and pulled it under the covers. I stuck my finger in it and licked it off. It was the perfect temperature, so I started to slurp it. It tasted amazing.

"I'm not gonna apologize for a stupid joke," he said.

"So you're admitting that it was stupid?"

"No, this is stupid. You're stupid."

"Then I'm not coming out."

"Fine by me," he said and left.

He was back an hour or so later and sat down on the bed.

"I won't do anything like that again, alright?" he said and sighed.

"And?"

"And nothing."

"Are you sorry?"

"You're gonna be sorry if you don't stop this soon."

"Why? What are you going to do to me?" I asked nervously.

"Nothing! Jesus! Look, I've searched the house earlier and I've found a couple of things you've missed, so I have every reason to be mad at you now. Do you really want me mad at you or should we just call it even instead?"

I thought about it for a second and then pulled down the blanket.

"What did you find and where? I was pretty thorough."

"I've found this in the little boy's room," he said and showed me a Snickers-bar. My eyes widened and I reached for it, but he held it over his head, so I got on my knees and tried to grab it. He pushed me back and I landed on my butt.

"Give it to me," I demanded.

"And reward you for dropping the ball? I don't think so. This is mine. You can watch me eat it later."

"I'll give you $100 for it," I said, determined.

"You still have money?" he asked, frowning.

"Yeah, it felt wrong to just throw it away."

"Damn, what other garbage do you have in your backpack?"

"It's not completely useless. I could've made a fire with it."

"You've never made a fire?" he asked with raised eyebrows.

"Well, once, on a tree, but it burned through the branches faster than I thought and fell down. It attracted monsters and I was stuck in that tree for five days and almost died."

"Jesus, you really are stupid."

"It wasn't my proudest moment."

"Yeah, no shit."

"So, $100 for the candy bar?"

"No thanks, what else you got?"

"I could wash your clothes for you."

"I've already done that, yours too by the way. You're welcome."

"Oh, thank you... I know. I'll cut your hair."

"Fine, what else?"

"That's not enough for you?"

"Nope."

"What more do you want?"

"You know what I want."

"No way, you can't have that."

"I can't? How about I rape the shit out of you to see if that's true?" My eyes widened with fear and they were starting to water, so I blinked a few times. I couldn't believe he would say something like that after what he had put me through the night before. I wasn't sure if he was serious or not, but I was still pretty scared. He sighed heavily and threw the candy bar in my lap.

"Thank you," I said meekly.

I leaned against the headboard, removed the wrapper, held it to my nose and then took a small bite out of it. I tasted so good, I closed my eyes and moaned softly.

For the next fifteen minutes or so I was in heaven. When I had eaten half of it I offered the rest to Troy.

"That's alright, chocolate isn't really my thing."

"Thanks... Hey, you seem to be in a relatively good mood today. What's wrong?"

"I'm just really hung over and my head is swimming."

"And that's a good thing?"

"Yeah, cause I can't really concentrate on how dire and hopeless life is."

"Your life isn't that dire anymore, you have me now, remember? You should jump for joy all day long because of that."

"Oh yeah, how about I make you jump?" he said and reached for me. I flinched, jerked back and looked at him fearfully. He frowned deeply.

"Stop being scared of me!" he demanded angrily.

"I'm sorry," I said nervously.

"I wasn't gonna hurt you! Jesus!"

"What were you going to do?"

"Come here." He said.

I scooted closer and he grabbed my stomach really roughly for a second.

"Oww!" I cried out.

"For fuck's sake, that was supposed to tickle!"

"It didn't, it hurt. It has probably even left a mark." I pulled up my shirt and there were in fact three red dots on my stomach. "Here, look," I said.

"I didn't mean to do that. And I wouldn't have if you weren't so fucking fragile."

"So this is my fault?"

"That's right."

"Have you always been like this, I mean, even before the world ended?"

"Like what?"

"A brute."

"Yeah and thank god for that or I'd be dead already. And so would you by the way."

"I know and I'm grateful, but I just can't imagine that it could've been easy being like this. You couldn't have had a girlfriend or even a boyfriend. No one would voluntarily put up with this kind of roughness."

"So what? It taught me to be by myself, one more thing that kept me alive. And what do you mean by 'boyfriend'? I'm not a fucking fag."

"You have to be at least bi."

"Hell no, I'm straight."

"But you want to have sex with me."

"So?"

"You don't think that's a little gay?"

"No, the way I see it, when it comes down to just getting off, a hole is a hole."

"How romantic... Yeah, I know, I will shut the 'f' up."

"That's right."

"So, have you even had sex before?"

"None of your fucking business."

"I see."

I sat up, facing him and crossed my legs. I tickled him softly on his side, but he slapped my hand away.

"What the fuck are you doing?" he asked, frowning.

"I'll teach you how to do it right."

"I don't need your fucking help."

"What if you meet a girl, maybe even the last girl on earth? Do you really think you could win her over by giving her bruises?"

"And what would you know about girls? You're a fag."

"Probably more than you. My best friend was a girl and we talked about boys all the time."

"Of course you did."

"Fine, but don't complain if we actually do meet a girl and she picks me. And then when you'll have to longingly listen to us making love all night long. I mean, I am gay, but you said it yourself, a hole is a hole."

"Fuck you!"

"Come on, let me make a human being out of you. You're already very strong and really handsome, so if we smooth out your rough edges a little you could be a real catch for some lonely, desperate girl."

"You think I'm good looking?"

"Yes, very. Well, at least with a proper haircut."

"Fine, what do I do?"

I tickled him again and this time he let me.

"Like this, you know?" I said.

"But that didn't tickle."

"Maybe you're just not ticklish. Try it on me, but very, very gently." He did, but it was still too rough and felt more like he was scratching me.

"No, a lot softer. You barely have to touch me, like when you were stroking my hair yesterday." He tried again and this time he actually managed to tickle me. I jerked a little and giggled. His eyebrows went up. "That was good. Now the lesson is over."

"Like hell it is," he said, grinning mischievously. He started to tickle me with both hands and I fell over backwards, laughing really hard.

"Nooo, stop it," I squealed, but he didn't and there was nothing I could do about it. I squirmed and laughed till he finally had mercy on me. When I looked up at him he was smiling.

"I should not have taught you that," I said, a little out of breath.

"Well, at least now I have something that isn't scary to threaten you with."

"You're not supposed to threaten me, period"

"Are you talking back to me?"

"No no, you're absolutely right, as always."

"Exactly." He leaned back against the headboard and I sat up.

"Did you find anything else?"

"Yeah, a deck of cards. How about we play some Poker after you've cut my hair?"

"Sure."

"Let's go then."

Troy found a chair and I cut his hair in the bathroom. It took forever, but I wanted to be thorough. I cut it pretty short and even shaved him neatly in the back. I was a little proud of myself and he seemed to like how it looked too, but didn't admit it.

Next we sat down in the kitchen and he taught me how to play Poker.

"Are you ready to play for real?" he asked after a few practice rounds.

"I think so."

"How about we make this interesting?"

"What do you have in mind?"

"Best out of three and if I win you have to give me a handjob."

"What do I get if I win?"

"What do you want?"

I thought for a second.

"I know. You can't curse for twenty-four hours and if you do anyway you have to apologize immediately."

"That's so fucking stupid."

"Take it or leave it."

"Fine, whatever."

We started to play and he won the first two rounds. I was getting nervous, but then I also won two games in a row, so we were even. The next round I was dealt a queen, a 9, a 7, a 5 and a 3. He kept all of his cards, which I took as a bad omen and when I exchanged four cards he grinned widely and made an obscene hand gesture.

"Ok, let's see them," I sighed and he revealed three 10's and two Aces.

"Full house, bitch."

I laid my cards on the table.

"Four kings. I win... B-i-t-c-h," I said and giggled. He frowned.

"What? No, you fucking cheated or something! That doesn't count."

"I barely know how to play this, so how could I possibly cheat? Don't be a sore loser. This so counts."

"Whatever."

"I think you just cursed, but you didn't apologize, which is weird since we had a bet and I'm pretty sure if you had won I'd be masturbating your penis right now."

"I'm sorry," he said, annoyed, and rolled his eyes.

"That's right."

"Come on, again. You're dealing."

"No thanks, I don't want to play anymore."

"Hey, that's not fair, I deserve a rematch."

"Ok, but if I win you have to walk around in women's clothes and make up for twenty-four hours. And I mean the full nine yards, with skirt and pantyhose and everything."

"Fuck you."

"Anything you want to add?"

"I'm sorry. Jesus Christ!" he said angrily.

"That counts as cursing too."

"No it doesn't."

"Fine. So, want to play? Because I'm on a roll right now," I said, grinning.

"No, you fu... fa... stupid queer!"

"That's not nice."

"Whatever."

"Did you find any other games we could play?"

"Yeah, but only kids' stuff."

"Might be fun too."

"We could die today. I don't want the last thing I do to be playing 'Hungry Hungry Hippos', you know?"

"Aww, they have that?"

"It's in the little boy's room. Knock yourself out."

"It wouldn't be fun playing it by myself."

"Then you're shit out of luck."

"I wish we could watch a movie."

"Well, we can't."

"That would be a really nice last thing to do before I die," I said sadly.

"Maybe one day, when all the freaks have died."

"When will that be?"

"Probably sooner than you think. Have you noticed how they smell? They're rotting, so it's just a matter of time till there's not enough flesh left to hold them together."

"I guess. How long do you think that will take?"

"I don't know. Another year or so? We just have to survive long enough and the world will be ours again."

"I hope you're right."

"When have I ever been wrong?" I hesitated. "Yeah, exactly," he said, grinning.

"I think I miss movies the most, and fresh fruit. What about you?"

"Beer, hands down, and I guess playing baseball."

"There are a couple of beers in the fridge, maybe they're still drinkable."

"And you didn't tell me?" he asked, frowning.

"I didn't want you to get drunk."

"I see."

He got up, went to the fridge and took out a beer. He opened it on the counter, held it to his nose and then tasted it.

"All right, that's what I'm talking about!" he said cheerfully.

"It's still good?"

"Yeah, it's perfect. Just what I needed."

"I'm happy for you."

"Thanks. Beer actually means a lot to me. I was a foster child, so I was always at the mercy of one douche bag or another and it made me feel really powerless. When I was sixteen I stole a beer at a store and went back to the boys' home. No one was in my room, so I sat down on the bed and drank it. I grew up with very strict rules and alcohol was like the forbidden fruit or something, so it felt like such a grown up thing to do. After a few sips I had a little buzz going and I pretended to be an adult already and that I was in control of my life and no one could tell me shit anymore. It was the best feeling and I made it my weekly ritual. I'd steal a beer and then, when I had a moment to myself, I'd sit down, drink it and daydream. It was the one thing I didn't hate about my life. And still to this day, whenever I drink a beer I feel better."

"That's so sad."

"Fuck you."

"No, I'm sorry, I didn't mean it in a bad way."

"Whatever."

"Hey, I have an idea. Why don't we read a book? That's almost as good as watching a movie."

"I'm not much of a reader."

"Then I'll read one to you. It'll be like listening to an audio book."

"I guess. Why not?"

We went to the living room together and looked through the book-shelf. It was mostly romance novels, a lot of cheap novelettes, but a few classics too.

"I don't wanna read a fu... stupid love story. They're for women," he said.

"I like love stories too."

"What's your point?"

"Very funny... How about this one?" I asked and held up 'The Time Traveler's Wife', which was a love story.

"It's about time travel, like 'Back to the Future'," I added, but that was a lie. I had seen the movie and it was nothing like 'Back to the Future', but I had to sell it to him somehow.

"It's not told from the point of view of the chick, is it?"

"No."

"And they have a time machine?"

"No, the guy just time travels."

"Is he some kind of mutant, like the X-Men?"

"Yeah, I think so."

"So it's a cross between 'Back to the Future' and 'X-Men'?"

"You could say that."

"Awesome. Let's read that one then."

I actually felt kind of bad for tricking him like that, but I thought maybe he'd enjoy the novel and thank me later for it. Probably not though.

We sat down on the couch, me cross-legged and him with his feet up on the coffee table. I opened the book and started to read it out loud.

After maybe two hours I took a break. We had made it through almost eighty pages and at least I was enjoying it very much. I managed to really lose myself in the story and forget the world around me for a while.

"So, what do you think?" I asked.

"I hate it."

"Oh, do you want to read something else?"

"No... I mean, whatever."

I grinned, but quickly turned serious again when he looked over at me.

"Hey, can I lie down and put my head on your lap? My legs are starting to hurt a little," I said.

"Sure."

I lay down.

"Is it ok if I rest my eyes for a while?" I asked.

"No, keep reading or I'll beat you." I looked at him wide-eyed and quickly picked up the book again. "Jesus! That was a joke! I've told you not to be scared of me anymore!" he said angrily.

"I can't just stop being scared because you tell me to."

"Why not?"

"Because that's not how feelings work."

"No, you just have to try harder."

"Or, you could stop threatening me, jokingly or not."

"Fine," he sighed, annoyed.

"Thank you." I said.

"Pull down your pants?" he sort of half asked half demanded.

"What? Why?"

"I'll make you feel good."

"You mean sexually?"

"Yes, now come on."

"No, I don't want that."

"You'll like it," he said and opened my pants. I tried to push his hand away, but couldn't.

"Please, don't do this, please."

"Shut up, you'll thank me later."

He pulled down my pants and underwear. I quickly covered my genitals with my hands and started to cry.

"Why the fuck are you crying?" he asked, frowning.

"Because you're trying to rape me."

"Rape you?! Are you shitting me?! I'm trying to give you a handjob! You should be thanking me!"

"You're trying to do something sexual to me without my consent, that's rape."

"Jesus!" He pushed me off his lap and I quickly pulled up my pants. It was really hard to button them, because I was shaking so badly. "I just wanted to do something nice for you, you know, to make up for scaring you!" he continued. That was kind of reassuring to hear and it calmed me down a little.

"That's not an excuse."

"Here, you can have the rest of my beers," he said and offered me his bottle.

"No thanks."

"Drink it!" he barked.

"But I don't like beer." He frowned deeply and smashed the bottle against the wall. I flinched and looked at him wide-eyed. He shot up and stormed out. A few seconds later I heard glass shatter in the kitchen. He came back and stared at me grimly.

"It's all gone! Are you happy now?!" he said.

"No?" I answered nervously.

"Of course not, I can't make you happy, I always do exactly the wrong thing!... I hate myself."

He was pale, breathing really hard and shaking. I was totally stunned by his outburst and I suddenly realized that he must've cared about me more than I thought. He looked like he was about to cry. I felt really bad for him, so I quickly got up and tried to hug him, but he pushed me away.

"Why the fuck are you hugging me?! Are you afraid I'll lose it completely and hurt you again?!" he asked.

"No, you're in pain, let me console you."

"I don't deserve that!"

"Of course you do."

"No, I don't!"

"I will hug you now and I'll hold on really tightly, so if you want to get me off of you, you'll have to hurt me. Do you understand?" I was finally barking an order at him. It felt good to be in control for the moment.

"I'm not gonna hurt you!"

"Good." I said, and I carefully took him in my arms. His heart was beating really fast, so I started to stroke his back and he slowly calmed down. It made me feel kind of powerful to help him for a change and I admired him for being man enough to let me. After about ten minutes he seemed much better, so we parted.

"Jesus, look at me, I'm a total mess. Your queerness must be rubbing off on me or something," he said.

"There's no shame in breaking down sometimes."

"Yes there is and we'll never speak about this ever or I'll..."

"What? Beat me?"

"No! Fuck! What's wrong with me?!"

"Well, you're used to acting before thinking I guess, which makes sense in this kind of world. But you're trying to change and that's what matters."

"You should hate me, you know?"

"But I don't."

"Maybe you have 'Stockholm syndrome' or something."

I giggled a little.

"I'm not your hostage or at least I hope I'm not."

"Of course not... Well, I don't know, I mean, I'd let you leave, but I'd probably follow you, to make sure you're safe."

"See, then you're more like my stalker than my captor."

"I'm not your fucking stalker!"

"I'm just saying, I don't have 'Stockholm syndrome'."

"That's good and I swear I'll be nicer to you from now on."

"I'm looking forward to it," I said, grinning.

"How about you read more of that stupid book to me?"

"You can admit that you like a love story, it doesn't make you any less of a man, you know?"

"Shut up and read already."

"Fine." I said and I laid down, put my head on his lap again and continued to read the book to him for a couple of hours. It was really fun and engaging and a great way to spend our time. We only took two breaks, one to go to the bathroom and another to rest my eyes for a few minutes.

When it started to get dark we quickly made ourselves something to eat and then went to bed. Troy had searched out some extra blankets, because he hadn't heated up the room this time. It was actually pretty cozy and definitely warm enough, but it was still very early and I couldn't sleep.

"Can't we cover up the windows and light a small candle, so we can read for a while?" I asked.

"No, we can't risk that. If we wanna stay here longer we can't attract any freaks."

"I guess that's true. So why don't we talk? Because I'm not tired at all yet."

"You know, sleeping without fear of getting killed is a privilege in this world."

"So you don't want to talk?"

"Whatever, I don't care."

"Ok, so, what did you do before the apocalypse?"

"I had lots of jobs, but I was a farm hand for almost a year before the world ended. I liked it. I also played baseball in a minor league. What about you?"

"I studied meteorology."

"What's that good for?"

"It's the scientific study of the atmosphere. I wanted to work for the National Weather Service someday or at least something like that."

"Isn't weather forecasting really inaccurate? I've read somewhere that the weather can't be predicted for more than three days. That doesn't sound like much of a science to me."

"It depends on how you look at it. The weather is just way too complex to predict it with 100% accuracy. If you knew how many variables factor into it you'd be amazed that it's possible at all."

"It's still stupid."

"Well, nowadays I guess knowing your way around a farm is a lot more useful."

"That's right."

"When did you know the world would end? Can you remember the moment?"

"Yeah, when I saw a freak for the first time. Before that I just couldn't believe it. The things they said on TV were just too crazy. I mean, it started in Africa, right? And they said that over two thirds of the population had died by an unknown contagion in just one day, but instead of staying dead most of them came back as mindless and extremely aggressive freaks and killed nearly all of the rest of the people. The next day it spread to Europe and the Middle East and over one billion people died within hours. It just sounded insane. And we stayed on the farm, so we didn't see the mayhem that had already broken out, the mass panic, the looting, people killing each other over supplies. When the phone and the TV went dead on the third day we drove into town. It was like a war zone, cars and buildings were burning and you could hear gunfire from every direction. That's when I saw a freak for the first time. He ran right in front of the car. I almost hit him, but he didn't even flinch, he just started attacking the vehicle. His eyes, they didn't look human anymore and the way he moved, there was something off about it. Next thing I knew a woman ran up to the door on the passenger side. She didn't see the freak, but he noticed her. He threw himself on her like an animal and bit half of her face off. Then suddenly another freak smashed into the door on my side. The window broke and he tried to sink his teeth into me. I punched him really hard and he tumbled backwards a few steps, so I quickly got the shotgun from under the seat and blasted him right in the chest. It didn't even seem to register with him, he just came at me again, so I stepped on the gas and drove off. That's when I knew the world was about to end."

Hearing all that made me respect Troy even more. It must've been traumatic to watch someone getting killed like that and then be attacked by a monster himself for the first time, but he had remained level-headed and made it out of there. I probably would've been scared stiff and not able to think straight anymore. Not Troy though, he was unflinching and always very focused. The only time I had ever seen him a little unsettled was after he had almost raped me accidentally in the living room.

"Wow, that's really horrible."

"No, that was just the warm up. It was nothing compared to what followed."

"I didn't know it was that bad."

"What do you mean? Where were you when all hell broke loose?"

"After the first reports I knew it would spread to the US in a matter of days, so I packed my things and drove as deep into the woods as possible. I figured, first of all, I'd be safer there and second, if I'd turn into a monster there wouldn't be any people around for me to kill. I stayed there all these months, hoping to hear something on the radio, that it was over or that they had found a cure, but sadly that never happened. Then, one day, I was looking for mushrooms when I suddenly saw a monster. It was like you said, it didn't look human anymore. I had never been so scared in my whole life and I ran for almost an hour, till I threw up, and then I climbed a tree and stayed there for four days. I spend most of that time debating if I should hang myself, but in the end I was more afraid to die than to live I guess."

"You know what? Climbing on trees was kind of smart. I should've done that too. I had to go through hell."

"Did you just pay me a compliment?"

"Don't get used to it, queer-ass bitch."

I giggled.

"Yeah, I know."

"Why did you go by yourself? Didn't you have any friends or family?" he asked.

"I did, but I had just started college, so they were hundreds of miles away. I knew I wouldn't make it there in time, so I called them and told them to get out of town. It was really emotional, because we knew it would probably be the last time we would ever talk to each other. We stayed on the phone for hours, cried a lot and finally said our goodbyes." A tear rolled down my face and I sniffled softly. Suddenly Troy grabbed me by the arm, which startled me a little, but he didn't pull and after a second he let go again.

"Come here," he said, so I leaned against him and he started to gently stroke my hair. It was surprisingly soothing.

"What about you? Did you have a chance to say goodbye to your loved ones?" I asked.

"No, there was no one I wanted to call really."

"What do you mean? Wasn't there anyone you were close to?"

"No. When I was six my father went to prison for killing my mother and I ended up in a foster family, where I was treated like a slave and they beat me more often than my father had. When I was fifteen I fought back and put the guy in the hospital. After that I spend some time in juvie and then stayed in boys' homes till I finally turned eighteen."

It made me so sad that he had such a horrible childhood and youth, and then, when things finally were looking up for him, the world ended. It was kind of tragic, but it explained a lot about his personality.

"I'm so sorry."

"Whatever, it toughened me up. It was like training for this nightmare."

"But you're not glad the world ended, are you?"

"Of course not, but before, I was nothing, just some reject with a criminal record. People looked down on me and treated me like shit all my life. But look at me now. I'm at the top, one of the last survivors on the planet. And not just by luck, I'm like a survival-machine. I've fought and I've won." He said the last part with pride and looked at me. I smiled at him in acknowledgement and he grinned back a little.

"I get it now, why it's so important to you to be respected and you're right, you've earned it."

"Exactly."

"How many people do you think are still alive out there?"

"No idea, maybe half a million world-wide, 25k in the US, if that. I only came across three other people in almost a year."

"Do you think there's a refuge somewhere?"

"Probably, but I don't know."

"I wonder what it would be like living in a place like that. I wouldn't be like before of course, but I bet if you were safe, had a job and a daily routine, it could almost feel normal again. That would be really nice, I think. I'd love to study something again, but I'd happily work too, as long as I could be useful in some way."

"If we'd ever find such a place, would you stay with me or would you rather share a room with some other queers?" he asked almost unsurely, frowning a little.

"Well, if I had to choose between living with strangers or living with you, I'd choose you."

"Cause I'm the devil you know, right?" he said disappointedly.

"No, even if we could live by ourselves I'd still want to see you every day."

He pushed me away.

"As some kind of courtesy or out of guilt, cause I saved your life?"

"No, I'd want to know what you're up to."

"But why?"

"Because I couldn't just ignore you. I don't think I feel guilty about it, but you did save my life."

"You know what? Go to hell," he said, annoyed.

"What did I say?"

"Plenty. Now shut up, we're done talking."

I suddenly felt bad for making it sound like I was only staying with him out of obligation. It was understandable that he became defensive.

"Troy, I..."

"I'm not saying it again," he said warningly, so I stayed quiet.

After maybe an hour of silence there were suddenly loud groans coming from outside. We both got up and looked out the window. There was a large horde of monsters walking by the house. It were maybe thirty of them, all moving very stiffly and ponderously, with some space between them. They didn't all groan at the same time, but alternately, almost like they were talking to each other. And it didn't sound aggressive either, but stretched out and kind of weary. It was really eerie.

"Get down," Troy whispered and we both went down on our knees, so our heads were below the window.

"What are we going to do?" I asked anxiously.

"There's nothing to do, except to hope that they're only passing through, cause if they stay we're pretty much fucked."

"Why are there so many?"

"I don't know, they like to follow each other. I think hordes likes these will become more common with time, which will be a real problem, cause no one can fight his way through that many freaks."

"I'm scared."

"Don't be, the house is pretty secure and if they get in anyway we'll be dead pretty fast."

"If they'll get in, could you shoot or stab me in the head please? I don't want to become one of them and kill someone."

"Just do it yourself, alright?"

"But then I won't go to heaven."

"Are you shitting me? That's what you're worried about right now?"

"Well, yeah, don't you want to go to heaven?"

"I don't care. The way I see it, hell would be like a vacation after living in this nightmare, so I can settle for that."

"Please shoot me in the head, ok?"

"I'll shoot you right now if you don't shut up already."

"Sorry."

"Let's go back to bed."

I nodded and we climbed into bed.

"Troy?"

"What?"

"Could you maybe hold me please?"

"Oh, so now that you need me I'm suddenly good enough for you?" he said challengingly.

"What do you mean?"

"I mean that I'm just a necessary evil to you and that you'll ditch me the first chance you get."

"That's not true, I'm staying with you because I want to, not because I have to."

"No, you'd die without me and you know it, so it's not much of a choice, now is it?" he said sulkily.

"What do you want me to say?"

"Nothing, just forget it."

It really bothered me that he felt that way. The truth was that I saw him as my fearless protector who'd always come through for me, and he had grown on me an awful lot already. I turned my back to him and pulled the blanket over my head. Suddenly he grabbed me by the waist and pulled me to him in one jerk. He closed his arms around me and held on to me really tightly.

"Troy?"

"What?"

"Please don't get mad, but you're squeezing me too hard." He instantly loosened his embrace. I turned around and cuddled myself against him. His body was really warm and I could hear his heart beating.

"Troy?"

"Jesus, what?" he asked, annoyed.

"Thank you," I said sincerely.

"Whatever."

We stayed like that for maybe one or two hours. Being so close to him was soothing, but I was still scared. Thankfully the groans eventually faded in the distance and I finally fell asleep.

CHAPTER 4

When I woke up the next morning I was still in his arms, he hadn't moved an inch. I carefully looked up and saw that he was already awake.

"Good morning. Why didn't you get up already?" I said.

"I wanted to let you sleep."

"Oh, thank you."

"Let's get something to eat, it's probably almost noon."

"Sure."

We got up, put some clothes on and then headed downstairs. After checking the house for monsters we went to the basement, to decide what we would have for lunch.

"What kind of soup do you prefer?" he asked.

"I don't really care for beans and I loved the tomato soup yesterday. What about you?"

"Yeah, that works for me."

We both took ours cans and went to the kitchen to heat them up. When they were ready we sat down at the table together. Troy ate very slowly and didn't seem to enjoy his meal very much.

"Don't you like it?" I asked.

"No, I'm just really sick of beans, that's all."

"Then why did you let me have the tomato soup?"

"Cause you said you loved it," he answered, frowning, like it was blatantly obvious.

"My germs are already in this one, but we can switch tomorrow."

"No, we won't, it's yours, all of it."

"But why? I don't mind."

"Cause I said so."

"But it's not fair."

"I don't care, now can we stop talking about this already?"

"Fine."

We finished our meal in silence.

"You can bake, right?" he asked.

"Why would you assume that?" I asked.

"You know, cause you're a... homosexual."

I would've been offended, but I actually knew how to bake a little and I appreciated that he didn't call me a queer or worse.

"I can make muffins, why?"

"I was thinking, we should celebrate, you know, that we dodged a bullet yesterday? I'll go out to hunt and you could bake muffins and tonight we'll have one hell of a feast. How does that sound?"

"Great, but what if the monsters hear the shot and the horde comes back?"

"There won't be any shots. I'm not stupid, I'll hunt for rabbits."

"How?"

"With a shovel. They live in holes, right? So I just have to find one, light a fire in it, cover it up, wait till the rabbit is dead and then dig it out."

That sounded like a ridiculous plan to me. I didn't know anything about hunting, but I had a hard time imagining that catching a rabbit could be that easy.

"Are you serious?"

"Yeah, I don't see why that wouldn't work. Do you?" He said the last part warningly and frowned at me.

"Well... No."

I decided against telling him what I thought about it, because I didn't want to risk not getting any rabbit on the off chance that he'd somehow manage to catch one.

"There you go."

"Be careful, ok?"

He nodded, went upstairs to get ready and left. I blocked the door and then busied myself with cleaning the house.

Later in the day I made the muffins, with cherries. They turned out pretty well. Just when I was starting to get worried I heard a knock on the door.

"It's me, open up," Troy said from the other side, so I let him in. He had blood all over his clothes, face and hands.

"What happened? Are you ok?" I asked, concerned. The thought of him being bitten suddenly crept into my head and really scared me. Because of him things had improved so drastically for me and for the first time in a long time I felt hopeful again. Losing him would've been devastating.

"Yeah, I was attacked, several times actually. There are a lot of freaks out there right now. I don't know what's up with that. I killed eleven of them and those were just the ones I couldn't get away from."

"You shouldn't have gone out there so soon. And for what? I could've told you that you wouldn't catch a rabbit," I said without thinking and my eyes immediately widened, because it was kind of an insulting thing to say and I was afraid he might react badly.

"So you probably think I'm an idiot for trying, don't you?"

"No?" I asked nervously.

"I have another question for you," he said. He took off his backpack and pulled out a pretty big, headless rabbit. "Who's the idiot now, bitch?"

"I don't believe it. You've caught one," I said, amazed.

"That's right."

"Can I still have some or are you mad at me now?" I asked unsurely.

"No, you can."

"Thank you," I said gratefully.

"Did you clean in here?"

"Yeah, why?"

"I was about to ask you the same question."

"I wanted the house to look nice, so we'd be more comfortable. Is that ok?"

"Sure... Do you know how to gut and skin this?"

"No."

"I'll show you in a minute, but first I'll fill the tub, so we can take another bath, cause I definitely need one."

"Ok, I'll help you."

"Alright, let's go."

We brought in the water together and then barricaded the door again. He showed me how to prepare the rabbit and when it was ready I seasoned it and put it in the oven. While it was roasting we went upstairs, got fresh clothes and checked the water in the tub. It was already comfortably warm.

"You can go in first," he said.

"Ok, thanks."

I looked at him unsurely and then slowly started to undress.

"I'll give you some privacy."

"Really?... I mean, thank you."

He nodded and left. I got in and sighed contentedly.

After soaking for a while I quickly washed my hair and my body and then dried myself off. When I was dressed I went looking for Troy and found him sitting right outside the bathroom.

"I'm done," I said.

"You could use a shave."

"I can do it later or tomorrow."

"No, come on, do it now, I don't mind."

"Are you sure?"

"Yeah, of course."

He got into the tub and I started to shave. I could see him lying there naked in the mirror. He had his eyes closed, so I snuck a peek from time to time. His body was really nice. He was pretty muscular and he had some hair on his chest, not a lot though, just enough to make him look manly. I didn't want him to catch me, so I finished up quickly and then left.

Downstairs I tried to set the table as fancily as I could, with candles, a tablecloth and napkins. I even opened a bottle of wine from the liquor cabinet. Next I boiled some rice and opened a can of peas. Right before everything was ready Troy appeared. He had shaved too and smelled of cologne.

"What's all this? Are we having a date I don't know about?" he asked, grinning.

"No, but I thought we wanted to celebrate."

"I'm just kidding, I think it's great," he said and slapped my shoulder really hard, which made me flinch. He frowned and held up his hands.

"Shit, did I hurt you? I didn't mean to, I swear," he said nervously and turned pale.

"No, you just startled me, that’s all." His frown deepened and he started to breathe more heavily, so I quickly hugged him.

"What the... What's that for?" he asked, surprised.

"No reason," I lied and he closed his arms around me. He didn't hold me too tightly this time. It was actually kind of nice. I breathed in his cologne and enjoyed the warmth of his body. The image of him lying naked in the tub kept popping up in my head and being pressed against him so closely seemed awfully intimate all of a sudden. My penis started to grow and I panicked a little, because I was afraid he might notice.

"I think dinner's ready," I said quickly, and thankfully he let go of me.

I took the rabbit out of the oven, put the rice and the peas in bowls and then set everything on the table. We sat down and Troy poured the wine. We both filled our plates and started to eat.

"Wow, this is the best meal I've had in a very long time and I mean even before the apocalypse," I said.

"I know, right? And we still have muffins for dessert."

"Oh my god, I almost forgot... Thank you so much Troy."

"What are you thanking me for? You made them."

"No, I mean for... everything I guess. I never would've thought I could be happy again. But right now I am, because of you, so thank you."

"I'm glad to hear that and right back at you."

He took his glass and held it up.

"To happy days," he said.

"To happy days," I repeated and we clinked glasses.

We didn't talk much for the rest of the meal. Afterwards we both had two muffins each. They were amazing and the wine went really well with them. We finished the whole bottle and by then it was already getting dark, so we decided to go to bed. Troy had to help me up the stairs, because I was pretty drunk. We undressed and slipped under the covers.

"Is the mattress floating by any chance?" I asked.

"Damn, you really can't hold your liquor, can you?"

"Look at me, I'm tiny and I drank half the bottle, so now there's at least as much alcohol as blood in my body, if not more. Probably more... What were we talking about again?"

He laughed.

"You definitely are drunk. Say, are you one of those people who get horny when they drink too much?"

My eyes widened.

"No? Why?" I asked nervously.

"No reason."

"Are you horny right now?" I asked.

"Don't worry, I won't try anything, I never will again. You have my word on that."

"Why?... I mean, thank you."

"Don't thank me, I shouldn't have tried anything in the first place."

"Why are you so nice to me today?"

"Cause you deserve it and I guess I'm happy too."

"I wish we could stay here forever."

"Yeah, me too. Maybe we can. Probably not forever, but for a long time at least."

"That would be nice... I'm getting really sleepy, I guess from all the food and the wine."

"Let's go to sleep then."

"Ok, good night."

"Night."

The room became quiet for a couple of minutes.

"You know, I could hold you again if you want. I mean, I wouldn't mind. Whatever."

"Yeah, sure." I smiled half-heartedly and then I cuddled myself against him and he closed his arms around me. I really enjoyed his warmth and being held by him and fell asleep pretty fast.

CHAPTER 5

The next morning I was still in his arms when I woke up. I didn't want him to let go yet, so I pretended to be asleep for another hour or so. I just felt so safe and snug being held by him. He smelled really nice too and I listened intently to his heart beating. When I finally looked up at him he grinned at me.

"Morning, sleepy head," he said.

"Good morning, how long have you been awake?"

"I don't know, a little over an hour maybe, so about as long as you."

I think I blushed.

"You knew I wasn't asleep? Why didn't you say something?"

"Why didn't you?"

"I was still too tired I guess," I lied.

"Are you hung over?"

"I'm feeling a little light-headed, but it's not too bad. What about you?"

"I'm alright."

"It's weird, I ate so much yesterday, but now I'm hungry again, more than usual actually."

"Let's eat then."

"Ok."

We got up, put some clothes on and went downstairs. Troy made coffee and then we sat down to eat a couple of muffins.

"Mmh, they're so good, if I may say so myself," I said cheerfully.

"Yeah they are," he replied, grinning, and ruffled my hair, but then he turned serious and quickly jerked his hand away. "You didn't consider that rape, did you? I mean, it wasn't sexual, so it's fine, right?" he asked nervously and I smiled at him.

"No, that was actually kind of sweet. It's only rape when you touch me, you know, down there, against my will, or if you make me touch you."

"Alright, got it."

"What do you want to do today?"

"I don't know, not much, maybe relax a little for a change?"

"Sounds good. How about we light a fire in the living room and finish the book?"

"Yeah, sure."

When we were done with breakfast Troy took care of the fire. Soon it was really warm and cozy in the living room and we made ourselves comfortable on the couch. He was sitting and I was lying with my head on his lap. I opened the book and we picked up where we had left off. After a while he started to gently stroke my hair. It gave me goose bumps, the good kind, and we spend the next couple of hours like that. The story became more and more fascinating and it was easy for me to immerse myself in it. Troy probably wasn't aware of this himself, but he'd always start stroking me for a few minutes whenever something romantic happened in the plot. I thought it was funny and pretty sweet, but I didn't want to embarrass him or for him to stop, so I pretended not to notice. I had such a good time though. Lying there with him, reading, getting tenderly touched, it was all very enjoyable and I was really happy.

In the early afternoon I became hungry again.

"How about we take a break and have lunch?" I asked.

"Sure. Why don't you make us something and I'll restart the fire? We can eat in here today."

"Good idea."

I went down to the basement and got two cans of soup. I was about to put them on the stove when I realized that there weren't any clean bowls left, so I unblocked the door, took a bucket and a knife and went outside to get water. I looked around, but luckily there weren't any monsters in sight. I used the pump as fast as I could and hurried back inside. I didn't block the entrance behind me though, because I figured I'd need more water soon anyway, to rinse everything off, so I just filled the sink and started to wash the dishes. Suddenly the door opened, which startled me so badly I thought my heart would stop beating. Two men entered cautiously and when the one in the front saw me he immediately pointed his gun at me. My eyes widened and I started to shake. I was so scared I even had trouble breathing.

"Oh my, what have we here?" he said. He had a beard and black, greasy, combed-back hair.

"Hello," I replied anxiously.

"Are you alone sweetheart?"

"Yes," I answered quickly.

"Dave, go search the house," he said to the other guy, who had a beard too and short, brown hair with a mullet in the back. He was also carrying a gun and he now headed toward the living room.

"What's your name sweetheart?" the guy who stayed with me asked.

"Cody?"

"Alright Cody. Why don't you turn around and bend over the counter for me, so we can get acquainted properly?"

"No!" I said in panic.

"You listen to me boy..." Suddenly there was a loud thud coming from the living room. "Dave?!...What's going on?!...Answer me?!" He quickly grabbed me, turned me around and took me in a choke hold from behind. Troy appeared in the door, holding up his shotgun. "Where's Dave, you son of a bitch?!" the guy yelled and pressed the barrel of his gun to my head.

"He's taking a nap. Now let him go and we'll talk," Troy said almost calmly.

"Lower your gun or I'll waste him right now!" Troy didn't respond and started to slowly walk into the kitchen.

"I swear to god I'll count to three and then I'll kill him!" the guy yelled warningly, and cocked his gun. "One... Two..."

"Alright," Troy said and lowered his shotgun. The guy aimed and shot him right in the chest without hesitation. He fell down sideways and disappeared behind the table.

"TROY!" I screamed and started to sob violently. The guy let go of me. He hit me in the head really hard and I dropped to the floor. He slowly walked to the table and looked around the corner. Suddenly a shot went off and his head exploded. I quickly got up and ran over to Troy. I couldn't even talk I was crying so badly. He was really pale and there was a small, but expanding blood stain on his shirt where he had been shot.

"Are you hurt?" he asked when he saw me and I shook my head. "Help me up." I did.

"Now take his gun, we have to check if there are more of them," he said. I picked up the gun and we went outside. There was a blue truck parked a couple of yards from the house, but there was no one else in sight, so we got back inside. Troy squatted down and checked the dead guy's pockets. Judging from his expression he was in a lot of pain and he was pressing his left arm against his stomach. After a few seconds he found a set of keys and got up. "Start packing, we're leaving in ten minutes," he said, but I didn't move, I was still in shock and sobbing violently.

"Listen to me, we'll be fine, alright? We just have to get out of here in case someone comes looking for those two fucks."

"You can't die," I whimpered.

"I won't fucking die, it looks worse than it is, trust me."

It looked pretty bad. The blood stain was as big as a basketball by now.

"It's my fault his happened. They must've seen the smoke."

"It doesn't matter. What matters is that you pull yourself together. I need you focused right now."

"I'm so sorry."

"For fuck's sake, snap out of it already or I will fucking die, alright?! Do you understand me?!" he yelled and I looked at him wide-eyed. "Move it!" he added and I quickly ran upstairs.

It was really hard to focus, but I managed to gather everything useful and ten minutes later the truck was loaded. Troy had bandaged his wound, but it looked like it was still bleeding.

"Do you know how to drive?" he asked when we were ready to leave.

"Yeah."

"Alright, let's go." We got in the truck. "There's a small path behind the barn, take it," he said.

"Ok."

We started to drive and I found the path. It was really uneven and Troy moaned in pain every time we hit a pot hole. Tears were streaming from my eyes and I could barely see. After a while we came to a road and took a left turn, away from the farm. There was the occasional abandoned car or monster, but thankfully nothing that really slowed us down. Troy's shirt continued to get soaked in blood, despite the bandage, and his eyes seemed to become heavier with every mile, which I knew was a bad sign. I floored the gas pedal the whole time, but the truck was old and just not very fast.

Maybe forty-five minutes later, which felt like an eternity, we finally came to a little town. Almost at the end of it I suddenly saw a house with an open garage, so I drove inside.

"What are you doing? We have to keep going," Troy said.

"No, we have to treat your wound or you'll bleed to death."

"It's not that bad."

"We're stopping here and that's final."

"Fine, now listen to me, if there are a lot of freaks in the house and they overpower me you don't try to save me, you run, alright?"

"No!"

"Cody, for fuck's sake, just do what I say!"

"No! You die, I die!" I yelled and then sobbed.

"Come on, let's go," he sighed and we got out of the truck.

I closed the garage door, and took our backpacks and two blankets with supplies and we entered the house. We were making our way to the stairs when suddenly a monster came out of one of the rooms we had just passed. Troy didn't hesitate and kicked its legs off the ground. The monster dropped to the floor and he stomped on it's head a couple of times till it burst. His face contorted with pain and he hunched down a little. I cried harder.

"I'm alright," he said reassuringly and straightened himself. He entered the room the monster came out of, so I followed him. It was a dining room.

"Can you carry a chair?" he asked and I nodded. We both took a chair and headed upstairs. We checked for monsters and then decided to settle in the bathroom.

"You can use the tub as a fireplace. Roll out my sleeping bag next to it," he said and I did.

He lay down and I blocked the door with one of the chairs and then tried to pull apart the other, but couldn't. I sobbed and desperately kicked it till finally a leg broke off. I kept at it and when I had enough wood I stacked it in the tub, opened a window and lit the wood. Next I kneeled down next to Troy and looked at him. He was pale and soaked in blood. Some of it had already curdled and smelled pretty bad.

"What do I do now?" I asked shakily.

"First you have to swear to me that you'll kill me if I die, so I won't turn into a freak."

"No!"

"Alright, then hand me my shotgun."

"Why?"

"So I can shoot myself in the head."

"No, please," I whimpered and cried harder again.

"Either you swear to do it or I'll do it right now."

I hesitated and he tried to get up.

"Ok, I swear," I said quickly.

"Good, now get your tweezers and the schnapps. You have to remove the bullet from my chest. And bring me the rod from the toilet paper holder, so I have something to bite down on."

I did what he had asked and he took off his shirt.

"Stick your finger in the wound, till you can feel the bullet, so you'll know where it is and then take it out with the tweezers," he said and took the rod in his mouth.

I quickly disinfected everything and then felt for the bullet. It was disgusting, but I was too afraid to care. Luckily it didn't seem to be very deep inside of him, so I used the tweezers. I couldn't get a hold of it right away, because my hand was shaking pretty badly, but after a few tries I finally managed to pull it out. Troy was sweating and breathing heavily. I covered his wound with a towel and applied pressure.

"Good job. Now you have to cauterize the wound, so it stops bleeding," he said weakly. I cried harder yet again and looked down despairingly. "Listen, I need you to be strong now, alright?" I nodded. "Find something made out of metal and put it in the fire till it's starting to glow and then shove it in the wound." I nodded, got up and took my fireiron out of my backpack. I disinfected it and then stuck it in the embers.

After a couple of minutes I checked if it was already glowing and it was, so I showed it to Troy.

"Do it," he said and bit down on the rod again.

I uncovered his wound. Tears were streaming down my face. I inhaled sharply and dug the fire iron into his flesh. It sizzled and the smell almost made me gag. Troy cramped up, moan loudly and passed out after a couple of seconds. I removed the no longer glowing metal and kneeled down to look at the wound up close. There was no more blood flowing out, which I took as a good sign. I cleaned it with alcohol, put toilet paper on it and then fixed it with duct tape. Next I wrapped him in the sleeping bag and covered him with two blankets, so he'd be warm enough. I sat down beside him and watched him breathe in and out. It took me a long time till I finally stopped crying.

When it got dark outside I gently laid my hand on Troy's chest, so I could feel it go up and down. I didn't move the whole night and in the morning, when he stayed unconscious, I started to panic. There was still some wood left, so I restarted the fire, to warm up the room. Around noon I cried for a while till I was too exhausted.

CHAPTER 6

In the afternoon I was about to lose all hope when he suddenly opened his eyes.

"Damn, you look awful," he said, grinning a little, and I burst into tears. "Hey, what's wrong?" he asked, concerned.

"I thought you wouldn't wake up again," I whimpered.

"How long was I out?"

"Over a day."

"But you stopped the bleeding, right?"

"Mm-hmm."

"Well, then there's no reason to cry, now is there?"

"I was so scared."

"I know, but you don't have to be anymore. I feel pretty awesome actually. You should burn me more often from now on."

I giggled a little.

"It was so horrible and smelled so bad."

"Yeah, but it felt great."

I giggled again, but then turned serious.

"I should cheer you up, not the other way around," I said sadly.

"Cheering you up cheers me up too, so there you go."

"Does it hurt really badly?"

"It's alright, but I wouldn't say no to a couple of painkillers."

I quickly got up and brought him the bottle with painkillers and some water. He took four pills and swallowed them.

"What do you want to eat?" I asked.

"I'm not hungry."

"Please," I pleaded and started to cry harder again.

"Alright, sure, whatever you want, just stop crying."

I nodded, wiped away my tears, got a can of tomato soup and opened it.

"Do you want me to feed you?" I asked.

"No, I'll manage."

"Ok." I said and handed him the can. He lifted his head a little and took a sip.

"Have you eaten yet?"

"No."

"And when was the last time you had something to drink?"

"I don't know, yesterday?"

"And why is that?"

"I just forgot, I guess."

"Go on then, eat and drink something, cause I wasn't kidding when I said you look awful."

"I'll have something to drink, but we don't know how long we'll be here and you need to eat more than me, so I'll save my share for you."

"Alright, if you don't eat, I don't eat."

"No, please."

"What if freaks show up and you're too weak to fight them off? Then we'd both be fucked."

"I'm too weak anyway," I said sadly.

"Bring me my shotgun."

"Why?"

"Well, if you won't protect me I might as well shoot myself right now, cause I'm not ending up as one of those fucking things."

"No, I'll protect you."

"Then you have to eat. So get another can or my shotgun, your choice."

"Ok, I'll eat," I said, defeated.

"That's right."

I got a can of bean soup and opened it, but before I could start eating it Troy took it from me and handed me the tomato soup.

"Troy, no!" I protested.

"Shut the fuck up and eat." He gave me a stern look, it wasn't that I was scared anymore really, but I more so didn't want to disappoint him.

"Ok." I agreed.

We finished our soup and then Troy closed his eyes. I leaned forward and gently stroked his hair. A tear accidentally dropped on his still naked chest and he looked up at me.

"What is it?" he asked.

"I'm so sorry this happened to you."

"Oh, that's right, you think this was your fault."

"It was, those guys found the house and got inside because of me."

"You're wrong, it was just really bad luck, nothing more."

"No, it was me and my stupidity."

"Look, the fire was your idea, but I agreed and I was even the one who started it."

"It was still my fault."

"Whatever... Hey, tell me something, how guilty do you actually feel? I mean, what would you be willing to do to make it up to me?"

"Anything... Well, almost anything."

"How about a blowjob?"

"Oh...Yeah, ok," I said hesitantly.

"Seriously?"

"Sure. Do you want me to do it right now?"

"Jesus Christ, I was kidding! You don't owe me anything and if you respect me you'll accept that, alright?"

"Ok," I said sadly and looked at the floor.

"Now, why is it so fucking cold in here?"

"I'm sorry, we ran out of wood."

"Have you checked the other rooms?"

"No, I was too scared to."

"It's getting dark anyway, so how about you get into the sleeping bag with me to warm me up?"

"But I have to keep watch."

"The door is blocked and I don't think freaks can climb stairs, so we should be safe. But bring me my shotgun, just in case."

"You're not going to shoot yourself, are you?"

"No."

I brought him his shotgun and then slipped into the sleeping bag. I cuddled myself against him and he laid his arm around me. I fell asleep pretty fast.

***

When I opened my eyes the next morning Troy was already awake.

"About time. Get up, I have to take a shit," he said.

"Oh, ok."

I climbed out and helped him up. I was scared to leave the room by myself, so while he was using the toilet I sat on the edge of the tub with my back to him and covered my ears. After ten minutes or so he tapped on my shoulder.

"How about you go next? We'll only get to flush once or twice, cause there's no more water pressure, so we should make it count," he said. I nodded and we switched places.

He wasn't actually watching me, but it was still really embarrassing doing my business with someone else in the room. I knew it was kind of silly, but I had always been very shy. I had gotten in trouble regularly in high school, because I never showered after gym class. Maybe it had something to do with the fact that I hit puberty pretty late. For a long time I was afraid other kids would make fun of me. For some reason that insecurity stuck with me.

When I was done I flushed and then we went searching for wood together. Right next door we found what looked like the room of a teenage girl, with posters of young actors and singers, stuffed animals and all kinds of other little things only a girl would collect. We took the mattress and all the drawers.

Back in the bathroom I broke everything into pieces while Troy started a new fire. After we had eaten we lay down on the mattress and just enjoyed the warmth. In the beginning I wanted to stay in a different room, but the tub was a great fireplace, because the metal would heat up like a radiator and now with a comfortable bed in it, it made perfect sense.

"Troy?" I asked after a while.

"Yes?"

"Why do you think those guys were like that?"

"Most people are inherently bad and now that there aren't any laws anymore nothing is holding them back."

"That can't be true. I bet there are still a lot of nice people out there."

"Nice gets you killed, you have to be tough to survive in this world."

"I survived."

"Well, you're the exception to the rule I guess.

"What if we'll find a refuge and there are only bad people?"

"If we'll ever find one I'll go in first and check it out, so you can run if something's not right."

"Or, we could just stay away and avoid other people altogether."

"That would mean it would only be us, probably for the rest of our lives."

"So?"

"A couple of days ago you said you'd ditch me if you had a choice."

"No, I said I'd prefer to live by myself, not that I wouldn't want to see you anymore."

"Would you still prefer to live by yourself, if you could?"

"No, not really."

"What changed you mind? Guilt?"

"No, you've changed, you started to be really nice to me and I enjoyed being with you, so if you don't go back to being mean I could totally picture myself staying with you for a long time."

"I see."

"Are you ok with it only being us for the foreseeable future?" I asked.

"Well, you're totally useless and you cry all the time, so I think I'd be better off without you."

I looked down disappointedly.

"Oh."

"Hey, I'm kidding. Well, at least about the 'better off without you' part."

"Really?"

"Yeah, so, together till the end?"

"Till the end."

"Damn, it feels like we just got married or something, except that I don't get to fuck you tonight."

"I'm sorry," I said sadly.

"Jesus, you have no sense of humor at all, do you?"

"But you do want to have sex with me, don't you?"

"No, not unless you're into it too."

"Exactly and I'm sorry I'm not."

"Whatever, I'll survive."

We stayed quiet for a while.

"What are we going to do? I mean, what's our plan, long term?" I asked.

"I don't know, we have a car now, so it'll be easier to get around. There are a couple more farms on the map from the delivery truck, we could check them out and then go from there. What do you think?"

"I think we should gather as many supplies as possible and then head to California."

"What's in California?"

"It's hot there and you said the monsters just have to rot long enough till they fall apart and die. So, everything rots faster when it's warm, which means they should die sooner in California."

"You're probably right. Why haven't I thought of that? It's a great idea, we should totally do that."

"So if we'll find another untouched farm you don't want to stay there again?"

"I don't know, we'll see."

"Ok and how long are we going to stay here?"

"A few more days maybe. I still feel a little weak."

"I wonder why the bullet didn't go through you, I mean, he pretty much shot you point blank."

"It was a very low powered gun and thank God for that or I'd probably be dead."

"Yeah, the bullet wasn't in very deep, which I thought was surprising."

"My shotgun definitely did more damage," he said and laughed, but immediately cramped up and moaned in pain. "Shit, maybe it's a good thing you don't have a sense of humor."

"I can be funny."

"Yeah? Tell a joke."

"Ok. The son says to his father: 'Dad, this boy in school keeps calling me gay.' The father asks: 'Then why don't you just beat him up?' and the boy answers: 'I can't, he's too cute.'" Troy laughed really hard and then cramped up again and moaned loudly, but couldn't stop laughing and his face kept contorting with pain. "I'm so sorry! I shouldn't have told you a joke," I said guiltily.

"It's alright, I asked for it, literally," he answered, a little out of breath.

"Still."

"I got one for you. What do you do if your girlfriend, or in your case boyfriend, starts smoking?"

"What?"

"You slow down and use some lubricant."

I laughed.

"That's kind of horrible."

"Let's get serious again, cause I don't wanna rip open my wound."

"Ok... Do you feel bad at all about shooting that guy?"

"No, should I?"

"I don't know, he was still a human being."

"He was worse than the freaks as far as I'm concerned."

"I guess."

"By the way, did you pack the book we were reading?"

"Yeah, but I left it in the truck, why?"

"How about we get it and you read it to me for a while?"

"So you do like it."

"No, I don't, I'm just bored."

"Oh, excuse me for boring you," I said sarcastically

"That's not what I meant."

"What did you mean then?"

"Why are you putting me on the spot?"

"I just think we should start being honest with each other. I mean, we used the toilet in front of each other earlier, so nothing should be embarrassing anymore."

"I'm not a homo."

"Straight guys can like romance novels too."

"Only pussies and I ain't no pussy."

"No, a lot of tough guys like them, but are too macho to admit it, which is a sign of insecurity if you ask me."

"Are you calling me insecure?" he asked, frowning.

"Yes, I am."

"You better watch it," he said warningly.

"Why do you even care so much what I think?"

"I don't."

"Yes, you do and I think it's because you have feelings for me. And that's also why you're being so nice to me, so I'll fall for you, but you're acting tough so I won't suspect anything."

"Are you shitting me with this?!" he asked angrily. "I'm only nice to you so you'll change your mind about letting me fuck you. And I don't have 'feelings' for you. You're like a talking dog to me! I'd have no problem putting you down if you'd stop doing what I want!"

"No, you could've forced me or even made me feel guilty and manipulated me into having sex with you, but you didn't, because you probably love me. And you said if I'd leave you'd follow me around, so if anything, you're like a dog."

He suddenly got up and glared at me.

"Get up!" he demanded.

"Why?"

"Do it!" he yelled, so I did.

"Now pull down your pants and underwear and bend over the sink!"

"No, please, I was out of line, I'm so sorry, it will never happen again, I swear," I said anxiously.

"Too late, I'm gonna teach you a lesson now, so next time you'll know your place."

I started to cry.

"No, please don't, please," I whimpered.

He grabbed me by the arm, pushed me against the sink, pulled down my pants and underwear and forced me to bend over. I was sobbing and shaking with fear. I heard him unbuckle his belt behind me and I waited for it to happen, but it didn't.

"FUCK!" he finally screamed and kicked what sounded like the water tank of the toilet, which broke with a loud crack, making water splash on the floor. I quickly pulled up my pants, went to the corner to my right, slid down with my back against the wall and hugged my legs to my chest. Troy was sitting on the closed toilet and was staring at the floor.

A few minutes passed. Suddenly he picked up his shotgun, which was lying next to the mattress, and put the barrel in his mouth. My eyes widened and I jumped up, ran over to him, grabbed it and tried to rip it out of his hands.

Chapter 7

A shot went off, but thankfully missed both of us. It hit the tube light on the ceiling though and pieces of broken glass came raining down. I quickly covered my face and hunched down a little. Troy let go of his shotgun and when I looked at him he seemed frozen and devoid of any emotions. He was just sitting there with sagging shoulders.

"What's wrong with you?!" I yelled, but he didn't react.

My ears were ringing so badly I felt a little disoriented, so I sat down on the mattress. After maybe twenty minutes he still hadn't moved, but my hearing had mostly returned to normal.

"Say something," I said and he glanced at me for a second and then looked down again.

"Why didn't you let me do it? I deserved it," he finally said quietly.

"No, you didn't, you lost your temper and you scared me really badly, but that doesn't mean you deserve to die."

"How can you defend what I did? There's no excuse."

"Because I know you're not a bad person."

"I have to make this up to you somehow."

"You could start by being honest with me."

"What do you mean?"

"No more pretending and acting tough. And I want to know where I stand with you."

"So you can use it against me?"

"Of course not. Don't you trust me?"

"I don't know. I don't trust anyone."

"That has to change. We have to learn to trust each other, because we'll spend a lot of time together and we're surrounded by danger and uncertainty, so there has to be at least one thing we can count on."

"I guess."

"I swear I'll never use anything you tell me against you and I'll always treat you with respect, as long as you do the same, which includes being honest."

"Alright." He said.

"Now, how do you feel about me?"

"What does it even matter?"

"I have to know what's going on in your head, so I'll know what to expect from you and how I should act around you. I'm already scared enough without having to worry about you all the time."

"You don't have to be scared of me. I'll never hurt you again."

"Until I say the wrong thing again you mean?"

"No, Jesus, I'd kill myself before I'd let anything like that happen again."

"And you think that wouldn't hurt me?"

He looked down and sighed.

"Just trust me, I won't let you down again, I swear," he said.

"Like you trust me?"

"For fuck sake Cody, I can't just trust you because you want me to. I'm not like you."

"Because you don't want to be."

"You're starting to piss me off," he said warningly.

"What are you going to do? Teach me another lesson?"

"No, Jesus, just cut it out already!"

"I won't, it's now or never. You have to prove to me I can trust you, I deserve that. And if you really can't, then I don't want to be around you anymore."

"We've been over this, you're not gonna leave."

"I will this time, if you don't give me any other choice."

"Fine, goodbye."

I got up and started to divide the food. It was difficult for me to see, because I was crying so hard. I wrapped everything in a blanket and tied it to my backpack. When I was ready I walked to the door and looked at Troy one last time. He was sitting there hunched, hugging his stomach and staring at the floor.

"Goodbye," I said quietly and left. I was half-way down the stairs when I heard him come after me.

"Wait. Stay, please," he said.

"I can't," I replied and continued to walk down the stairs.

"I love you, alright?" I stopped and turned around.

"Are you IN love with me?"

"I'm not a... gay."

"That's not what I asked."

"I don't know. I really don't."

"Would you like to kiss me?"

"What? No... I mean, I guess I would, if you wanted me to."

"Why do you hate it when I cry?"

"Cause it rips me up inside."

"Why did you try to hurt me earlier?"

"You were really getting under my skin and pushed me into a corner. And then you said I'm like a dog and I just lost it."

"You said I'm like a dog to you first."

"I was only trying to protect myself."

"What about now?"

"I don't give a shit anymore. I'd rather be your bitch than to let you go."

"I see."

"You got what you wanted. Are you staying now?"

"Fine, but no more 'Mr. tough guy', ok?"

"Sure."

I went back to the bathroom with him.

"This place is a mess," I said.

"I'll clean everything up."

"I'll help."

"Alright, but not the glass, I don't want you to cut yourself."

"Fine."

For the next twenty minutes or so we cleaned as best as we could, restarted the fire and had something to eat.

"We should put the hamper in the other room and use it as a toilet," I said.

"It's permeable."

"But you can sit on it and we could look for some plastic bags, put one inside when we use it and then throw it out the window when we're done."

"I guess...We should also piss out the window."

"Yeah."

"It's getting dark... I have an idea, I'll be right back."

"Where are you going?"

"You'll see."

He took the shotgun and left. I suddenly felt some anxiety building up in me, but I wasn't sure what I was scared of… being by myself or that something might happen to him. Thankfully he was back maybe five minutes later with the book, a roll of trash bags and two flowerpots. He closed the window and then extinguished the fire with the soil from the pots.

"Now it'll stay warm a little longer," he said.

"That's nice, but it'll still get chilly tonight. I wish we had a heater."

"We can just warm each other."

"I'm not sure I'm ready to be that close to you again."

"Oh, yeah, I understand."

"I'm not doing that to punish you. You know that, don't you?"

"Even if you would punish me, I'd deserve it."

"I can't argue with that."

"How do you feel about me? In general I mean, am I still just a dog to you?"

"Of course not. I care about you, a lot, but I don't have feelings for you, if that's what you're asking."

"Yeah, no, whatever... Do you think you could ever... You know what? Never mind."

"If I could ever fall for you? It depends on how you'll treat me, but yes, it's possible."

"How long do you think that might take?"

"How long did it take for you?"

"I don't wanna say."

"Come on, please?"

"Fifteen minutes."

"What? But I must've been unconscious for at least that long."

"Yeah, but then you woke up... I knew I was in trouble the second you opened your eyes."

"Aww, that's so romantic." He frowned at me. "In a very manly kind of way I mean," I quickly added.

"Don't fucking patronize me."

"Sorry."

"We should get some sleep, I'm pretty beat."

"Me too."

We lay down, he in his sleeping bag and I covering myself with the two blankets. I missed being close to him and it took me a long time to fall asleep.

When I opened my eyes the next morning I looked over to Troy, but he was gone and the door was open. I panicked a little, quickly got up and went looking for him. First I checked the next room and when I entered I saw him sitting awkwardly on the hamper with a roll of toilet paper in his hand. He noticed me and frowned.

"Do you mind?" he asked.

"Sorry," I said sheepishly and returned to the bathroom.

I started a new fire and maybe five minutes later Troy appeared and blocked the door behind him with the chair.

"Morning," he said, grinning.

"Good morning."

"I'm hungry, how about we share a can of pears?"

"Sure. You must be recovering well if you're getting your appetite back so soon."

"I guess, I'm definitely feeling much better already."

When the fire was burning we sat down on the mattress and he opened a can of pears.

"You could use a shave," he said and touched my jawline. His fingers lingered and he stroked the stubble on my chin for a couple of seconds. Suddenly he realized what he was doing and quickly jerked his hand away.

"Shit, I shouldn't have done that, I'm sorry," he said, frowning, and I grinned a little.

"It's ok, don't worry about it."

"We could use one of the bottles of water to get cleaned up, you know?"

"Do you really think we should waste our water like that?"

"We'd feel better afterwards, so it might be worth it."

"I wouldn't mind washing my hair and changing at least my shirt, underwear and socks."

"There you go."

We finished eating and then Troy went downstairs to get fresh clothes while I used the 'toilet'. We filled the sink with water and I let him wash himself first, then it was my turn. When I was done I called him back in.

"You were right, I feel much better now," I said.

"I know. And you look like a million bucks."

"Thanks, you too," I replied, smiling.

"Thanks."

"Hey, did you wash your feet too?" I asked.

"Of course not, do you really think I'd let you wash your hair in the same water I washed my feet in?"

"I guess not. Come on, I'll do it for you if you want."

"Sure."

I laid a towel on the floor and Troy took off his socks and put one foot in the sink. I lathered it, massaged the soap in and then rinsed it in the water. I did the same to the other foot and then kneeled down to dry them.

"Thanks," he said.

"Your toenails are awfully long. I have nail scissors, let's cut them."

"Alright, if you want."

I got my nail scissors from my backpack. We sat down and he leaned against the tub. I laid his foot on my lap and started to carefully cut his toenails.

"This is nice, you grooming me I mean. Can I do you next?"

"Ok."

When I was done with his, I let him do mine.

"Oww, you're cutting too deep!" I cried out.

"No I'm not."

"Oww!" I cried out again, pulled back my foot and looked at my big toe. When I squeezed it, it started to bleed a little. Troy turned pale.

"I didn't mean to do that," he said nervously.

"I know, it's ok."

"No, it's not, I hurt you, again. I can't believe this!"

"It's no big deal. It's harder to cut someone else's nails, you just have to get used to it. Come on, give it another shot," I said and put my foot back on his lap.

"I'll never touch you again, ever."

"Please? I trust you."

"Maybe you shouldn't."

"But I do. Come on, I know you won't hurt me again."

"Fine," he said hesitantly and took a hold of my foot. He was extremely careful this time. After every cut he looked up at me and I smiled at him reassuringly. When he was done he sighed heavily.

"Thanks, great job," I said cheerfully.

"Does your toe hurt badly?"

"No, not at all," I lied. It was actually still throbbing a little.

"Good."

"Now do my fingers."

"No way, that was like defusing a bomb or something. I can't handle any more of that."

"Ok, then let me do yours."

"Alright."

"Cross your legs please."

He did, I crossed mine too and scooted closer to him till our legs were touching. I laid a towel between us, took his hand and started to cut his nails.

While I was busy he suddenly leaned forward for a second. At first I didn't think much of it, because I figured he had just adjusted his position, but then he did it again and lingered for a moment. That's when it dawned on me that he had probably just smelled my hair. I lifted my head and frowned at him. He looked at me wide-eyed, like a kid caught with his hand in the cookie jar. My face relaxed and I smiled at him. He seemed relieved and grinned back sheepishly, it was kind of adorable. I finished his hands, did mine and then cleaned up.

"Now we're as good as new," I said cheerfully.

"Well, except I'm still injured and you're crippled."

"But we're alive, clean, neat, warm, and full. That's a lot to be happy about."

"I guess... Do you wanna read to me for a while?"

"Sure."

He lay down straight and I sideways on the mattress. I used his waist as a pillow and started to read. From time to time he would stroke my hair and we completely forgot to eat lunch. Late in the afternoon we finished the book. I was really moved by the ending, even though I had already known what would happen.

"That was bullshit," Troy said.

"I thought it was sweet."

"No, the word is 'bullshit'. What kind of ending is that? Total bummer."

"Next time we'll read something with a happy ending, ok?"

"How would we know?"

"I'll read the last couple of pages first, to myself of course."

"No, that would spoil the whole story for you, so I'll do it."

"I saw the 'Twilight' books in the other room. They'd keep us busy for a while and the ending is awesome."

"Hell no."

"Why not?"

"I saw the trailer for one of the movies once and you have to either be a teenage girl or really fucking gay to like that shit."

"So I'm really f-ing gay and like a teenage girl apparently?"

"No, I'm just saying, it's not for me. And it wasn't meant as an insult, hell, for all we know you could be the gayest person on earth."

"I am not the gayest person on earth," I said indignantly.

"How do you know? You could be the last of your kind."

"That's improbable."

"But not impossible."

"Anyway! Let's read 'Twilight'."

"No thanks."

"Are you afraid you might like it?"

"I won't!"

"Fine, there's also 'The Hitchhiker's Guide to the Galaxy'."

"What's it about?"

"I don't know. It's a comedy as far as I know."

"Sounds good, let's give it a try."

"We should eat something first and then we can read till it gets dark."

"Sure."

While I took care of the fire Troy got more flower pots and a drawer. We heated up two cans of corned beef and had dinner. Afterwards we read 'The Hitchhiker's Guide to the Galaxy' for a while. We had to laugh out loud a couple of times, it was great and it seemed like the book was meant to be read with company. When it got dark Troy extinguished the fire with soil again and we lay down to sleep. I wanted to be held by him, but only scooted close enough so our arms were touching.

Chapter 8

When it got dark Troy extinguished the fire with soil again and we lay down to sleep. I wanted to be held by him, but only scooted close enough so our arms were touching.

"Do you think we'll make it to California?" I asked.

"Yeah, a lot of roads will probably be blocked and it'll take a long time, but I'm sure we'll get there."

"Have you ever been there?"

"No, you?"

"No, but I bet it's great."

"Yeah, I've been thinking, we could find a nice, big house on the beach somewhere, plant a garden, go out fishing and really build a life for ourselves there, you know?"

"I'd like that. Do you think we could get a dog too? Maybe if we'd find puppies somewhere?"

"A dog barks, which could get us killed."

"What if we teach him not to bark?"

"You can't do that. Dogs bark."

"That's probably true. Maybe we can get one when all the monsters are dead."

"You don't want a cat?"

"Not really."

"We could breed jackrabbits. They'd probably get tame enough over time that you could pet them and play with them."

"But then we couldn't eat them anymore."

"Why not?"

"You can't eat pets."

"It's the apocalypse Cody, you can eat anything."

"But I want at least one for myself."

"Alright, sounds reasonable."

"Tell me more about our life together."

"Well, when we've found a place that's remote enough we'll have to secure it, build a fence, maybe booby traps and then we'll probably spend most of our time scavenging, looking after our garden, hunting, stuff like that. But on the weekends we'll do nothing. We'll get clean, sleep in, have elaborate meals, go swimming, maybe even surfing, and read. We'll do that for a while and then, when all the freaks are gone, the real fun begins. We'll move near a city, get the most expensive sport cars, go on joy rides and make trips where we stay in fancy hotels and mansions. Also, we'll get the best projector and sound system for our house and every night we'll watch movies and play games."

"That does sound like fun. We could also get a bunch of designer clothes and just throw them away when they're dirty. And we could go to museums and art galleries and take whatever we like to decorate the house with."

"Sure."

"I wish we were already there and could do all that stuff. But we don't even know if we'll make it there alive or if the monsters are really going to die someday. And even if they do there are still bad people out there who want to kill us, that won't change."

"We just have to take it one day at a time, hope for the best and plan for the worst. It's pointless worrying about things that are out of our control and who knows, maybe we'll get lucky and everything will turn out fine."

"That's a good attitude and you're right, we should stay positive."

"Exactly."

"We'll need maps. What if we don't find any?"

"It would probably be easier to find a navigation system, I mean, the satellites should still work, right?"

"I don't see why not and that would be really great."

"We should still look for regular maps though, just in case. A lot of people have one in their glove compartment, at least one for the state they live in."

"We'll need a lot of fuel too."

"Yeah, we should start sucking it out of every car we come across."

"That's going to be gross."

"Don't worry, I'll do it, no need for both of us to get nauseated."

"Thanks."

"Sure."

We stayed quiet for a while.

"Hey, what do you think it's like to suck a dick?" Troy asked.

"I don't know, I think it could be exciting, stimulating your partner and giving him pleasure like that. But it's also work, kind of, that's probably why it's called a job. And if you're only on the giving and never on the receiving end it won't stay exciting for long either."

"Do you think it tastes like piss?"

"No, not if it's clean. It probably doesn't really taste like anything, unless there's pre-ejaculate. I've heard that it tastes a little bitter and salty, but not necessarily bad. I don't pre-ejaculate by the way."

"I'm not sucking your dick!"

"I'm just saying, and just so you know, if we ever become a couple I won't do anything you're not willing to do for me too."

"But you're gay, I'm not, so that's not fair," he said, frowning.

"That doesn't mean I should have to do all the work and get relatively little pleasure in return."

"I could give you handjobs."

"That's not the same as oral sex."

"Fine, be like that."

"You know what, after what you've put me through I'll probably never want to do anything sexual with you anyway, so this argument is moot."

There was a pause.

"You're right, I'm sorry."

"It's ok."

We didn't talk for a few minutes.

"When do you think you'll be ready to travel?" I finally asked.

"Maybe in a day or two, why? Are you eager to get back out there?"

"No, not really, this is not too bad."

"It sure beats sleeping in the truck and keeping watch all night. I'm not looking forward to that."

"Yeah, me neither... Hey, do you think we could grow bananas and strawberries in California?... Uh, and peaches... And honeydew melons... And huckleberries."

"I'm afraid we'll have to be a little more practical than that. I mean, we'll have to water all those plants somehow and it never rains in California, so we'll have to prioritize. We could maybe grow one fruit if we had to."

"Or we'll just find a place with a well or a river close by, then we could grow all the fruits we wanted, couldn't we?"

"Sure, but that's easier said than done."

"I'd do anything to eat fresh fruit salad again."

"Alright, then that's our new main goal in life, making sure you'll get fresh fruit salad again someday."

"I know, I'm being an idiot, I'm sorry."

"Why would you say that?"

"Because you were making fun of me and you're right, it was stupid."

"I wasn't making fun of you. Everyone needs a goal in life and growing enough fruit for a salad is as good as any."

"What about what you want?"

"You can't play baseball with only two people and all the beer will have gone bad soon, so there's no point in looking for any."

"Well, we could still get a glove, a bat and some balls and have fun. We could even go to Dodgers Stadium in LA and play there. And if the monsters are gone we'll get you one of those machines that shoot balls at you. We could also find a library and get a book on how to brew your own beer. It can't be too hard and that way you'll be able to drink so much you'll get a belly."

"I guess, that would be kind of cool."

"See? We can both be happy."

"Alright, but fruit salad comes first."

"Fine, if you insist."

"I do."

"We should pray to God, you know? Ask him to look out for us."

"I think God stopped looking out for us a while ago."

"I guess, but it still can't hurt to ask."

"Knock yourself out."

I folded my hands and silently prayed to God. I asked him for forgiveness for our sins and for him to guide and protect us. It felt a little weird, because I hadn't talked to God since I was a child. My parents weren't religious, but my grandmother was and whenever I stayed with her overnight we would say a prayer together before I went to bed. After a while I started doing that at home too, but then she died and it became too painful, because it reminded me too much of her, so I stopped.

"Ok, I prayed for the both of us," I said when I was done.

"Great, now we'll have nothing to worry about anymore."

"Maybe not, I mean, he can't be very busy at the moment and we're good people, so it's possible that he'll help us."

"If that belief lets you sleep better at night, more power to you."

"Speaking of sleeping, are you tired yet?"

"Yes, very."

"Oh, I'm sorry, why didn't you say something?"

"I like listening to you talk."

"That's sweet, but I'll let you sleep now, good night."

"Night."

I lay awake for maybe two hours, but I didn't mind, it was peaceful. We had a full moon and it was light enough to see a little. I watched Troy's chest rise and fall and listened to the silence. He looked so vulnerable when he was sleeping. At one point his face started to twitch a little, which made me think that he might be having a nightmare. It wouldn't have been surprising after what he had been through. Not knowing what else to do I gently stroked his arm, hoping it would help somehow. Sure enough the twitching stopped and I grinned to myself proudly.

In the morning I was woken by the smell of fresh smoke and when I opened my eyes I saw Troy leaning against the tub, watching me.

"Man you're a sound sleeper, I've been up for over an hour," he said.

"I'm tired," I replied drowsily.

"Come on, you have to help me break drawers. I want the fire to be burning all day."

"Ten more minutes, ok?"

"Fine."

I closed my eyes and what felt like ten seconds later I was shaken by Troy.

"Let's go, rise and motherfucking shine, bitch," he said cheerfully. I moaned and pulled the blanket over my head. "Do I have to tickle you awake? Cause I will," he added.

"No no, I'm awake," I said, alarmed, and quickly sat up.

"What do you want for breakfast? Prunes or pears?"

"Pears please."

"Here, have some coffee," he said and handed me a steaming cup.

"Thanks, just what I need."

"I know."

I took a sip and felt how the hot beverage slowly filled my body with warmth. I closed my eyed and moaned softly. When I opened them again Troy was smiling at me.

"You seem to be in a good mood," I said.

"Yeah, I've decided that we're gonna have fun today."

"We are?"

"Yes, I've found a board game we could play and we still have the book to finish and enough wood that it'll stay nice and cozy in here."

"What board game?"

"It's called 'Pandemic', you play it co-operatively and have to save the world from ending."

I giggled.

"I think we've already lost that game."

He frowned.

"Yeah, I guess it was a stupid idea."

"No, it sounds fun, let's play it."

"Alright, but business before pleasure, we have to break this stuff first."

"Sure."

I finished my coffee and we shared a can of pears. After I had used the 'toilet' we started to break drawers together.

"These too?" I asked and held up a speaker.

"Yeah, why not."

Troy took it and opened the back with his knife.

"Holy shit, look what I've found," he said and showed me a small plastic bag with what looked like green tea in it.

"What's that?"

"It's weed. There's even a pipe in here."

"Oh, you mean marijuana?"

"Yeah, we're gonna get so fucked up."

"I don't know if I want to take drugs and I don't think you should smoke that either, you're still recovering after all."

"Weed is good for you. They prescribe it to people with cancer. If anything, I'll heal faster."

"But that's not medical marijuana."

"Weed is weed. Come on, don't be a killjoy, getting high is a lot of fun."

"Ok, I'll try some."

"That's the spirit."

We finished breaking wood, put some on the fire and sat down. He was leaning against the tub and I was sitting in front of him with my legs crossed. He filled the little pipe, lit it, took a long drag, and inhaled the smoke deeply. He held it in for a few seconds and then blew it out. He cleaned the pipe, refilled it and handed it to me. I took a long drag too, but had to cough as soon as the smoke entered my lungs.

"I feel dizzy," I said.

"Me too."

"Do you want to play the game now?"

"Sure."

I set up the board between us and started to read the instructions out loud.

"Do you get it?" I asked when I was through. He looked at me with a surprised expression. His eyes were bloodshot and seemed really small, which made me grin.

"Get what?"

"The game, I just read the instructions to you."

"Oh, you read that to me? I wasn't listening."

"Who else did you think I was reading it to?"

"I don't know, to be honest, I thought you were just talking crazy."

"Do you want me to read it again?"

"Read what again?"

"The instructions?... For the game?"

"Oh, yeah, right on."

I read them to him again.

"And, do you get it now?" I asked.

"Not at all, whatsoever, period. What about you? You've read it twice now."

"No, I'm stumped."

"You know what we should do?"

"No idea."

"Dance."

"But we don't have any music."

"I could sing a song and you could dance to it."

"Go for it."

He started to sing, completely out of tune.

"Bye bye American pie, I drove a Chevy into a levee, but it was totally dry and the good old boys drink whiskey and cry, this will be the day that I die, this will be the day that I die...Wow, this song is such a bummer."

We both laughed, but he immediately held his chest and frowned.

"Does it still hurt a lot?"

"No, I'm holding my chest cause I'm so patriotic," he said, grinning.

"Do you want me to kiss it better?"

"Sure, but no tongue, alright?"

I giggled, leaned forward and gently kissed his chest. I lifted my head a little and our faces were only an inch or two apart. I closed my eyes and our mouths touched. His lips were softer than I imagined them to be and to my surprise he kissed me very tenderly. He was really retrained and applied just the right amount of pressure. It felt pretty exciting, but I knew we shouldn't be doing this. I didn't want our relationship to become sexual, at least not as long as I didn't have feelings for him, so after a few seconds I pulled away and sat back down.

CHAPTER 9

"That's weird, I'm really hard right now, but I'm not gay at all. How is that possible?" he said.

"Well, maybe you're only gay for me and otherwise you're totally straight."

"Yeah, and there's prison-gay, you know, when guys get attracted to other guys cause they haven't been around women for so long, right? Maybe I'm apocalypse-gay, for you."

"It's possible."

Suddenly he poked his wound and moaned in pain.

"Shit, it hurts so bad, I think it's time to kiss it better again. You can even use your tongue this time if you want," he said and I frowned.

"Don't do that. And I'm not kissing you again. I shouldn't have done that in the first place."

"That's so cruel, teasing me like that, you know?"

"I blame the drugs."

"You know what we should do?"

"Eat? A lot? I'm so hungry."

"Sure, we can do that too, but first we should smoke more weed."

"So you can take advantage of me?" I asked, grinning. He blinked a few times and looked down.

"I won't touch you, I swear on my life," he said sadly, which made me frown.

"Hey, I was only kidding. You can touch me if you want."

He looked at me and raised his eyebrows.

"I can?"

"Not down there and no kissing, ok?"

"Alright, got it."

"Let's smoke more weed."

"Oh, look who's tasted blood."

"Well, it is kind of fun and it's not like we can get addicted or anything."

"That's right."

We both smoked another pipe and then decided to lay down. We didn't talk for a while and just stared at the ceiling.

"What are you thinking right now?" Troy finally asked.

"I'm wondering how hard it is to kill an elephant."

"Wow, I never would've guessed that."

I laughed.

"I know."

"Do you feel like getting up?"

"No, I feel kind of wonderful."

"You are wonderful."

I smiled.

"Oh, you." I said. I turned on my side and hugged his arm. "Are my eyes as bloodshot as yours?" I asked

"I don't know."

"Look at me then."

He did and grinned.

"Yep, totally bloodshot... Do you want me to kiss them better?"

"No, but thanks."

"Are you still hungry?"

"Very much."

"I'll make us something."

"That's amazing."

"I can't get up though."

"Oh no."

"Yeah."

"Hey, what if we'd get attacked by monsters while we're like this?" I asked.

"Maybe if we'll hold our breaths they'll think we're dead and leave."

"How long can you hold your breath for?"

"Five minutes."

"Really? Wow... Wait, that can't be true, you'd die."

"Oh, you meant without dying? Ten seconds then."

I laughed really hard.

"That's not very long."

"How long can you do it for?"

"Let's find out," I said, inhaled deeply and held my breath. After a while I exhaled and gasped.

"How long was that?" I asked.

"How the fuck should I know?"

I giggled.

"Why do you always have to curse?"

"No fucking idea."

I giggled again.

"Why don't we take a little nap?"

"Great idea."

I closed my eyes and fell asleep shortly after. When I woke up I was still hugging Troy's arm and then I noticed that he was watching me.

"Finally," he said.

"How long have you been up?"

"Half an hour maybe."

"I don't feel as high anymore, but I'm still hungry."

"Let's eat then."

We restarted the fire and heated up two cans of soup. When I tasted it I moaned with pleasure.

"This is so good. It's like I hadn't eaten in days or something," I said.

"Yeah, weed does that."

We finished our soup in silence.

"What do you wanna do now?" Troy asked.

"Duh, smoke more weed of course."

He grinned.

We both smoked another pipe, then we lay down and I hugged Troy's arm again.

"You know what our new life goal should be?" I asked and I could feel him trying not to laugh.

"To smoke weed every day?"

"Yeah, no, well, yeah, but no. Our new goal should be to grow marijuana and I mean like an acre or something."

"We couldn't smoke that in a lifetime."

"Speak for yourself."

He laughed, tensed up and moaned.

"We can't be stoned all the time," he said. "This is an exception, but we have to stay sharp or we won't survive for long. I mean, we shouldn't be stoned right now."

"Yes we should, let's smoke some more."

After yet another pipe my brain felt totally fried and could barely keep my eyes open.

"Troy, are you still there?" I asked.

"I don't understand the question."

I laughed really hard, but then I thought of something and turned serious.

"Troy! Get my backpack!"

"You're kidding, right?"

"No, I don't think so... What was I just saying again?"

"Get my backpack."

"Why?"

"I don't know."

"Wow, we're really high right now... But we're on the ground, so we're technically low, but we're on the second floor, so we're high, but low, but high."

"You're freaking me out."

"Yeah, me too."

We stayed quiet for a while.

"Someone has to put more wood on the fire," Troy said.

"Oh no."

"I'll do it."

"That's amazing."

He sat up, went on all fours, crawled to the pile of wood and carried a couple of pieces to the tub. Next he got my backpack, dropped it in my lap and lay back down.

"No, please, I don't want to leave, please," I said, alarmed, and quickly hugged his arm.

"What? Who said anything about leaving?"

"You brought me my backpack."

"You told me to, remember?"

"Oh... Thanks then, I guess."

"You're welcome."

I pressed myself against him, wrapped my legs around his and laid my arm over his stomach.

"You're hard," Troy said.

"What? No... Oh yeah, I am. Weird."

"Wanna do something about it?"

"Like thinking of something gross?"

"No, like getting off."

"That's way too much work and I'd probably fall asleep half-way through."

I felt him laughing a little.

"I could do all the work if you want."

"No, I'm too high to decide something like that right now. Let's just cuddle, ok?"

"Alright, sure."

"Thanks."

"Man, I'd kill for a bag of chips right now."

"Uuh, we still have a can of spinach, we could eat that. It's like chips in a way, isn't it?"

"It's nothing like chips, at all."

"That's very true."

I could feel him laughing again.

"Hey, wait a minute, we have canned potatoes, oil, spices, oil, a pen, canned potatoes and a camping stove, we could make chips ourselves," he said.

"Just listening to you list all the thing we'd need was exhausting."

"Yeah, you're right, bad idea."

"Troy! Oh my god, get my backpack, quickly!"

"It's lying next to you."

"That's amazing."

I turned around and searched my backpack till I found the half-eaten Snickers bar and showed it to Troy.

"Look what I've found," I said cheerfully and he grabbed it right out of my hand.

"Thanks."

My eyes widened and I quickly pulled out his knife.

"Give it back to me right now or I'll cut you," I said warningly and he laughed, tensed up and pressed his hand against his wound.

"Cut this," he replied and grabbed his crotch.

"I will."

"I bet you this candy bar that you won't."

"Fine, eat it, but I'll never speak to you again," I said, pouting. I turned my back to him and curled up in a ball.

"You're not crying, are you?"

I just held up my middle finger.

A few minutes passed and then he suddenly reached over me and put the candy bar next to my head.

"I was only kidding, you pouty-ass bitch," he said. I took it and turned around.

"Well, to punish you I will now eat it in front of you and when I'm done I'll belch in your face." He laughed really hard, but immediately winced and inhaled sharply.

"I still have the weed, you know?" he said.

"Oh... Hey, let's share this candy bar, ok?"

"That's alright, you can have it."

I frowned.

"But eating this will be amazing."

"Yeah, enjoy."

"No, we're sharing this and that's final."

"Fine, but you're getting the bigger piece."

"Hush now."

I split the candy bar evenly and handed him the lower half. I took a small bite out of my piece and closed my eyes.

"Oh Jesus, that really hits the spot," Troy said.

"Yeah, it's like an orgasm in my mouth."

"You can have an orgasm in your mouth any time you want, you know? You just have to blow me. Won't taste as good though."

"You're a pig," I said indignantly.

"I was kidding, Jeez, you're such a prude."

I wanted to object, but he kind of had a point there.

We ate the candy bar and then I cuddled myself against Troy again.

"How much weed do we have left?" I asked.

"Four pipes worth maybe."

"We should smoke all of it before we go to sleep."

"I agree."

"What time is it?"

"It's a quarter past no fucking clue."

"Don't curse," I said and slapped his chest playfully. He tensed up and moaned.

"What the fuck?"

My eyes widened and I lifted my head.

"I am so sorry," I gasped.

"It's fine, just don't do that again, alright?"

"No. Never," I said and gently stroked his arm.

We both smoked another pipe to ease the pain. I took Troy's hand and we just lay there in silence for a couple of minutes. Suddenly I smelled something foul.

"Did you just break wind?" I asked.

"I don't know, something happened down there, but I'm not sure what. Felt good though."

"Maybe I should break wind too."

"Go for it."

I tried, but couldn't.

"It didn't work."

"Bummer."

"Yeah."

"I need to take a nap, I think."

"Me too."

I fell asleep shortly after. When I woke up I felt almost sober again, so I restarted the fire and watched it burn for a while. When there were only embers left I opened two cans of meat loaf and heated them up. I shook Troy awake and we ate. We had prunes for dessert and then dozed around till it got dark, smoked the rest of the weed and went to sleep.

CHAPTER 10

The next morning my head felt heavy, like I had taken too many sleeping pills the night before and it hurt a little. I just lay there, daydreaming about the future, till Troy opened his eyes an hour or so later.

"Good morning, do you feel as bad as I do?" I asked.

"Probably worse, since I've been shot recently and all."

"You're right, poor thing," I said and stroked his arm.

"It was worth it though, wasn't it? I mean, we had fun yesterday, right?"

"Yeah, it was a really great day and I guess being hung over is a fair price for that."

"Do you still want to grow an acre of weed?" he asked, grinning.

"I'm not planning to become a drug addict, if that's what you're asking and it's unlikely that we'll find seeds anyway, but in case we do I don't see why we shouldn't grow a couple of plants."

"Yeah, I guess."

"I don't feel like getting up, can't we just stay in bed all day?"

"Sure, why not, but I think tomorrow it's time for us to move on."

"Do we have to?"

"Well, right now we might still have enough supplies to last us till we get to California and that would be one thing less to worry about, so we should take advantage of that."

"That's true. Ok, tomorrow then, so let's really enjoy today, because we don't know when we'll be this comfortable again."

"Sounds like a plan. I'll take care of the fire and you can pick something for us to eat in the meantime."

"Ok."

After breakfast we lay down, I cuddled myself against Troy and we just enjoyed the warmth of the fire. We dozed off occasionally and around noon I felt drowsier than I had hours before. We heated up some soup and ate.

"You should kiss me," Troy said when we were both finished.

"I should? And why is that?"

"To see if I'll get hard."

"What if you do?"

"Then we'll know it wasn't just the weed."

"But I don't feel like kissing you right now."

"Just come here for a second." he said. He leaned forward and pressed our lips together. It felt kind of nice and even though I knew it was a bad idea I couldn't stop myself. I kissed him back. After a couple of seconds he suddenly tried to slip me his tongue and I immediately backed away.

"You can't just kiss me, that's very rude," I said, pretending to be indignant, so he wouldn't kiss me again. I wanted him to, but I didn't have feelings for him yet and kissing could quickly lead to more. That was a problem for me, because I was shy, even a little prudish and I also considered myself a romantic, so having sex casually wasn't an option.

"It's not like I held you in place or anything. And you liked it, just admit it." he replied, grinning.

"Well, I didn't hate it. What about you?"

"Me neither. I'm definitely apocalypse-gay for you."

"Good, now that we've established that there's no reason for us to kiss again anytime soon. Understood?" He leaned forward, but I held him back. "Troy, no!" I said warningly.

"Aww, come on, don't be like that, let's have some fun."

"No, if anything is going to happen between us I want it to be when I'm ready and on my terms, ok? You owe me that, don't you think?"

"Alright, sure."

"Thank you."

"Wanna read to me?"

"Ok."

I got the book, we lay down together and Troy took me in his arms. I read to him for a couple of hours and we reached the end just when it was about to get dark. We had another meal and went to bed.

In the morning I felt saddened by the fact that we had to leave and a little frightened by the things that were waiting for us up ahead. We ate a can of pineapple together, packed, and carried everything to the truck.

***

After studying the map and determining the fastest ways to all the farms on it, we headed out. Since it would've been painful for Troy I was driving. The truck was old and so loud it was hard to hear each other, so we didn't talk. It was a snowy, cold, but sunny day and thankfully none of the roads were blocked. Half an hour later we arrived at the first farm, but it was burned down. The next one looked untouched, but there were monsters everywhere and they started to walk toward us from all directions, like someone had just rang the dinner bell, so we quickly moved on before they could surround the truck. On our way to another farm we passed a train station.

"Let's check it out! We might find a map in there!" Troy yelled.

"Ok!"

I pulled into the parking lot. We got out and entered the station. Inside there was a big room with stores on the sides and doors at the end, leading to the tracks. In the middle there were a couple of benches and a monster was sitting on one of them with his back to us. We walked up to it and Troy got ready to stab it in the head. It was a female monster. She had a big hole in her stomach and a dead newborn was lying in front of her, with a blood trail behind it. Next to her was a suitcase she was holding on to with one hand. When she saw us she didn't move or make any sound, she just watched us with her black eyes. It was really eerie.

"Yikes," Troy said, disgusted.

"Why isn't she attacking us?" I asked nervously, peeking at her from behind Troy's back.

"I don't know, I've never seen anything like it."

"Do you think she ripped it out or that it clawed its way out itself?"

"Does it really matter?" he asked indifferently.

"I guess not. What do you think is in the suitcase?"

"Let's find out," he said and raised his knife again to stab her in the head. The monster showed no sign that she cared.

"Wait!... Do we have to kill her? She's not doing anything," I said with some sadness in my voice.

"She's a freak Cody," he replied disapprovingly and frowned at me.

"Please?" I begged and looked at him puppy-dog-eyed. He lowered his knife.

"Fine," he sighed, "but if she comes after us you have to kill her yourself, alright?"

"Ok, thank you," I said in relief.

There was one of those tags you get at an airport on her suitcase.

"It says here her name is 'Antje'. How weird, she's probably from Europe. Maybe people from there don't become aggressive when they turn into monsters and that's why she doesn't attack us," I said.

"How nice for them. Can we move this along?"

"Yeah, sorry. Antje, please don't attack me, ok?"

Troy raised his eyebrows and looked at me like I was crazy.

I kneeled down and slowly pulled the suitcase away from her. Thankfully she didn't seem to mind. I opened it and thoroughly searched it. Except for a toiletry bag there was nothing useful in it.

"Check the front pocket," Troy said, so I did and sure enough there was a map of the entire state in it.

"How great is this?" I asked cheerfully.

"Well, it's a start. Now let's go."

I got up.

"Thank you Antje. I'm sorry about your baby. Goodbye."

"Jesus, why don't you give her a farewell kiss?" he said and shook his head a little.

"What? She's a very nice monster."

"Whatever."

We searched the stores, but didn't find anything useful, so we went back to the truck.

The last farm on the map was very near the road and when we got there a monster came out of the front door, so we figured the place had already been looted and wasn't worth the trouble.

"What are we going to do now?" I asked.

"Let's just head west and play it by ear from now on."

"Ok. We'll need gas soon, we're almost running on empty."

"There's a one-horse town thirty minutes from here, we should find some cars there."

"Let's hope so."

"Hey, you asked God to help us, so what could possibly go wrong, right?" he said without any sarcasm in his voice, which surprised me.

"I guess," I replied, grinning.

We made it to the town after an hour or so and fortunately there were no monsters in sight. We started to break into cars till we found a fuel canister in one of the trunks. Troy insisted that only he would suck the gasoline out of the tanks. At his first two tries he spat out a whole mouth full, it was really gross and I felt bad for him, but I was also grateful that I didn't have to do that. We refilled the truck and kept heading west.

"It's getting dark soon! We should look for a place to sleep in the next town!" I yelled.

"No, we shouldn't stop or it'll take us forever to get to California!"

"But I'm tired from driving all day!"

"Then let me take over!"

"But that'll be painful!"

"It would be more painful to clear a house full of freaks!"

"Fine, but when do we eat?! I'm hungry!"

"How about right now?!"

"Ok!"

I pulled over and we heated up two cans of mixed vegetables on the camping stove. After we had eaten we relieved ourselves and got back on the road.

"Maybe you should try to take a nap!" I yelled.

"Yeah!"

He lay down, put his head on my lap and closed his eyes. I kept driving till two o'clock in the morning and then Troy took over. The truck was too loud, so it was almost impossible to sleep and when the sun came up I was exhausted. Around mid-morning we stopped to have breakfast. It was really chilly and snowing a little. The sky was cloudy and dark.

"We can't keep going like this or one of us will fall asleep and drive into a tree," I said.

"We just have to get used to this. It'll be fine."

"No, I'm totally beat and you don't look so good either. We should rest, at least for a couple of hours."

"This fucking truck is too damn slow, so we have to push on or we'll run out of supplies half-way to California."

"Please?"

He sighed.

"Alright, we'll rest, tonight."

"Thank you."

We ate a can of fruit and then continued our journey. In the afternoon we ran low on gas again, so we decided to look for cars in the next town. Troy had only filled half the tank when two monsters walked out of a building. He barely managed to kill them and then three more showed up, so we fled. The town after that had only four houses and one burned out car.

"What are we going to do?" I asked. "We'll cross the state line in about twenty miles and since we don't have a map for that state we have no idea when we'll get to another populated area again. We should go back."

"No, we're not going back."

"But what if we'll run out of gas?"

"Then we'll be fucked."

"Exactly."

"It'll be fine, God is on our side, remember? Well, at least on yours, but that should be enough."

"But you said you think God doesn't care anymore."

"He cares about you, so we will find gas, you'll see."

"Are you so sure because you think I'm an angel?"

"I was drunk when I said that."

"People tend to tell the truth when they're drunk."

"Let's just say I'm not completely ruling it out, alright?"

"I'm not an angel Troy."

"We're not going back."

I didn't agree with him that we should keep going, but I trusted him and if he was sure we'd make it then that was good enough for me.

"Fine."

Troy kept driving till past midnight and then we finally stopped. After we had something to eat we lay down, he on the seats and I on the floor, since I was smaller. I fell asleep right away. I was woken with a start by a loud banging. Troy and I got up at the same time and when I looked outside there was a horde of monsters, dozens of them, all around us. I immediately started to shake with fear. They must've seen us move or maybe they could smell us, because more and more of them walked over to the truck, groaning aggressively, and pushed against it. Troy quickly got in the driver's seat and started the engine. At the same time the window on the passenger's side shattered and two monsters reached in and tried to grab me.

"TROY!" I screamed in terror. He put the truck into gear and stepped on the gas. We drove off, but one of the monsters was still caught in the window.

"Troy!" I yelled, totally panicked.

"Kick it!"

"No, it'll grab me!"

"Hold on!"

I quickly wrapped myself around him and he stepped on the brakes. The monster was thrown off the window and Troy accelerated again.

My whole body was shaking and I even had started to cry without noticing it. I held on to Troy for dear life. Thankfully he didn't seem to mind. After maybe twenty minutes he suddenly stopped the truck.

"No, what are you doing? Keep going," I said anxiously.

"There are no freaks around as far as I can tell and we need to fix the window, it's fucking freezing in here."

"No, please."

"It'll take five minutes and then I'll hold you for a while, alright?"

"Ok," I said sadly.

I stayed inside while he cut a rectangular piece out of my tarp and duct taped it over the window. When he was back I climbed on his lap and clung to him. He laid his arms around me and stroked my back till I finally stopped shaking.

"All better?" he asked.

"Yeah, thank you."

"We should go."

"Ok, but I'll drive. It's my turn anyway and you need some rest."

"Are you sure?"

"Yes."

I took over the wheel, he lay down and we got back on the road. The sun came up an hour later and stung my eyes. I was overtired and my hands and feet were really cold. I wanted to take a break, but I was too afraid to.

Around ten I saw a group of monsters up ahead, blocking the road, so I slowed down. There was a path leading into the woods on the right. Not knowing what else to do, I took it. Maybe half an hour and a couple of turns later we were completely lost. The worst part about it was that we were almost out of gas, so I stopped the truck. I was so scared and desperate, I couldn't think straight anymore and started to cry. Troy opened his eyes and frowned.

"Hey, what's wrong?" he said, concerned.

"We are going to die, because of me," I whimpered and he sat up.

"Where the hell are we?" he asked.

"I don't know."

"Why are we in the middle of the woods?"

"There were monsters on the road."

"So?"

"I was scared."

"You should've told me," he said matter-of-factly, but to my surprise not in an accusatory tone.

"I'm sorry."

"It's alright. And we're not dead yet, so please stop crying. Can you do that for me?" he said reassuringly, which really helped me to calm down a little. I had been so afraid he would be furious with me, but instead he was very understanding and focused, like he always was when it mattered.

"Ok," I answered quietly and wiped away my tears.

"Let's go. I'll drive."

We switched seats and he started the truck. We followed the path, but there was no end in sight, only the thick forest as far as the eye could see. Suddenly the engine stuttered and I was so overwhelmed with guilt and fear again that I couldn't hold back my tears any longer.

CHAPTER 11

Suddenly I saw something in the distance that looked like a gate. As we got closer I realized that it stretched across the whole path and seemed to be the entrance to an estate. We drove up to it and Troy went outside to open it. I folded my hands and prayed silently. We passed through and he closed it again behind us.

After five minutes or so we came to a small hill. The truck stuttered a little on the way up and I tightened my grip till my knuckles turned white. When we reached the top a big farmhouse came into view. My eyes widened.

"Thank God," I gasped.

The estate was vast and surrounded by forest, but there was not much on it. There was maybe an acre of open field and a few single trees spread across it randomly. Everything was covered with a thin layer of snow, which made it look really peaceful.

We parked in front of the house and got out. When we opened the screeching door we were hit by a wave of a stench so foul we had to pull up our shirts to cover our mouths and noses. We started checking all the rooms and right before we went into the one next to the stairs a monster came out and jumped Troy. He fell down on his back and the monster landed on top of him. He needed both arms to fend it off, so he couldn't stab it. I kicked it in the stomach, but that had no effect, so I took a hold of it around its waist and pulled it off of Troy. The monster didn't like that. It turned around and grabbed my leg with its bony hands. I screamed and it tried to bite me. Right before it could sink its rotten, black teeth into me Troy stabbed it in the head and it stopped moving. I freed myself from its grip and backed away. Troy got up and looked at me with concern.

"Did it get you?" he asked.

"No. You?"

"No."

He walked over and hugged me.

"You're shaking," he said.

"Yeah, well, they're still monsters to me and getting attacked by one is really terrifying."

"You just saved my life, do you realize that?"

"So what? You saved mine right after and a couple of times before that."

"It doesn't make it any less of a big deal, especially since you're so scared of them. So thank you."

"My pleasure."

"We should look through the rest of the house."

We parted and went into the room the monster came out of. It was the living room and there was a partially eaten and heavily decomposed body lying on the floor. We quickly covered our faces again, but I started to gag anyway and ran outside. Troy joined me a few seconds later.

"Are you alright?" he asked.

"Yeah, I just need a minute."

"Let's see what we find out here."

We walked around the house. There was a gas tank in the back, a well nearby and a shed right next to it with a generator and cubical tank in it.

"Do you think that's gasoline?" I asked.

Troy opened the valve of the tank, held his finger under it and then smelled it.

"Yes it is."

"That's so great! This will get us to California three times over. We really lucked out. I bet we'll find food in there too," I said cheerfully.

"I'm not so sure it was luck."

"If I were an angel, don't you think God would've brought me up to heaven instead of letting me live in this nightmare for almost a year now?"

"Maybe this is how you earn your wings, like a rite of passage, you know?"

"Wouldn't I know that I'm an angel?"

"Apparently not."

I rolled my eyes and shook my head a little.

"I'm not an angel, that's ridiculous Troy."

"No, it makes perfect sense, kind of. First you survived for so long on your own, which is a small miracle and then you met me. And I was a horrible person, but you've changed me. I'm a new man now. That's like divine intervention or something. And I have feelings for you, even though I'm straight, that's another miracle right there. Now this. How much more proof do you need?"

"There's a logical explanation for all of that. Calling me an angel is just crazy, can't you see that?"

"Not more crazy than believing in God or Jesus. And I don't see how that's a bad thing. Everyone has to believe in something. And this doesn't affect you negatively in any way, on the contrary, so why would you try to convince me that I'm wrong?"

"Because you are."

"Can you prove that? Or is it just something you believe very strongly?"

"No... Troy!"

"There you go," he said, grinning, and kissed me on the nose, which made me giggle.

There was also a barn about two hundred yards away, but it was locked. We got two shirts out of the truck that we used to breathe through and went back into the house. We found a pantry under the stairs. It was filled with food, some of it rotten, but still enough to last us a very long time.

"Look, there's jam... and honey," I said excitedly.

"And peanut butter."

"Where?"

"There."

He pointed at a jar. I quickly grabbed it and stuffed it in my jacket pocket.

"That's mine."

"You can keep it in there, it's not like I'll eat it now that I know you want it so badly," he said, grinning.

"No, I'll carry it around, so I can smell it whenever I want."

"Will you let me smell it too?"

"Maybe."

He laughed and shook his head.

We checked all the rooms upstairs, but there were no more monsters.

"First things first, we have to seal the door to the living room and then air this place out for a couple of hours. We should also throw out all the curtains, rugs and anything else that soaks up odors."

"Ok, you do the door and the windows, I'll do the rest."

"Alright."

We went to work and maybe thirty minutes later we were done. We decided to have lunch, so we got in the truck with the camping stove and heated up two cans of soup.

"We could stay here, you know?" I said. "It's isolated and fenced, so we'd be safe from monsters and there's enough space and water to grow anything we want. It's unlikely we'll find a better place in California. What do you think?"

"The freaks might already be dead in California, so we could be a lot safer there, cause the fence probably couldn't keep a whole horde of freaks out. Besides, the house reeks of death and I'm not sure we'll ever get rid of that smell completely. That's something to consider too."

"That's true, but I hate this truck and being on the road was horrible."

"Let's just wait and see how the house airs out first, alright?"

"Ok."

When we were both finished with lunch I pulled out the peanut butter, opened the jar and smelled it.

"Oh my god, this is amazing," I said and held it to Troy's nose.

"Yeah, nice."

I took some on my spoon, put it in my mouth, closed my eyes and moaned softy. I let it melt on my tongue and savored the taste for a couple of minutes. When I finally swallowed I scooped up some more and offered it to Troy.

"No thanks, enjoy," he said and I frowned.

"But you have to try it."

"No, it's all yours."

"If you believe I'm a 'divine being', shouldn't you do whatever I tell you?"

He laughed.

"You'd like that, wouldn't you? And no, you're too kind for your own good, so I have to protect you from yourself."

"But it would make me happy if you'd have some too."

"It'll make you even happier when you'll eat it yourself."

"If you try it I'll give you a kiss."

"Why the hell is this so important to you?"

"Because everything is better when you can share it with someone and this is one of few pleasurable things left in this world, so it would be a waste not to share it." He frowned, reluctantly took the spoon and licked off the peanut butter. "Amazing, isn't it?" I asked, smiling.

"Yeah, I guess," he answered and grinned. I leaned forward to kiss him, but he stopped me. "You don't have to do that," he said.

"Maybe I want to."

He let go of me and I leaned in. We kissed for a couple of seconds and then I backed away. We looked at each other and smiled.

"We should find the keys for the barn. I want to know what's in there," I said.

"It's probably just a tractor or a bunch of dead animals."

"Or maybe lots of hay. We could build a big pile and then jump on it from up high."

"And why would we do that?" he asked, grinning.

"Cause it's fun?"

"If you'd break your other leg, we'd be totally fucked. I couldn't even carry you around and we don't have a wheelchair or even crutches."

"That's true. So no hay jumping," I said disappointedly.

"We should hope for seeds and tools we can till a field with."

"I guess. Come on, let's find the keys."

"Alright."

We got out of the truck and entered the house. The stench was still intense and nauseating. We found a bunch of keys hanging in the kitchen, so we took all of them and went to the barn. After figuring out which one fit in the lock, we finally opened the doors. My eyes widened when I saw what was inside.

"Holy shit!" Troy said, dumbstruck.

"Yeah, exactly."

"Do you still think you're not an angel?"

"I really don't know anymore... It looks brand new."

"It probably is."

We walked to the only door on the side of the RV. It was open, so we went in. It was pretty spacious, there was a kitchen with a wood burner and a closet on the left, leading to a bedroom in the back and on the right, across from the kitchen, there was a table and then the bathroom. There was also another bed above the driver's cabin.

"This is fucking awesome. We could use the bedroom for storage, the closet for wood and sleep up here," Troy said excitedly.

"Yeah, it's perfect. Try if it'll start."

"It won't."

My heart fell and I frowned.

"Why not?"

"Because the battery is long dead."

"Oh no. Can't we recharge it somehow, with the generator maybe?"

"Probably, but that would make too much noise. We could use the battery from the truck though, if we had the right tools."

"Then let's find some."

We didn't have to look far. There was a little shed adjacent to the barn. It was filled with tools. We took what we needed, removed the battery from the truck and installed it in the RV. We went back inside and Troy put the key in the ignition. I folded my hands and prayed silently. He turned the key and the engine stuttered, but wouldn't start. He tried it a few more times, but it didn't work.

"Please," I whispered and suddenly the RV roared to life. I sighed in relief and we smiled at each other, but then I thought of something and turned serious.

"Does this run on gasoline?" I asked.

"Yeah, what else?"

"Diesel?"

He raised his eyebrows.

"Oh shit. That would be such a pain in the ass to find."

We went outside and looked, but it didn't say 'Diesel' on the lid or the cap.

"Thank God," I said.

"Yeah, thank God."

"We should load everything in here and fill the water and the gas tank, so we'll be ready to go in case monsters or bad guys show up. And we should sleep in here tonight."

"I agree."

We drove up to the house and decided to get the tank from the shed into the RV first, which turned out to be really difficult, because it was extremely heavy. We used a rope, a shovel, a wheelbarrow and a car jack and it involved a lot of leveraging and dragging. Poor Troy had to endure so much pain to help me, but I couldn't have done it on my own. Next we cleaned a rain barrel, put it in our storage room and then gradually filled it with water from the well. After that we searched the house thoroughly and brought anything useful over. I looked through the RV too and found a travel atlas with maps of every state in the glove compartment. Last we refilled the water for the sink and the shower, and the gas tank, and drove back into the barn. We were both sweaty and totally exhausted, but happy with what we had accomplished. There was just enough time left for us to take a bath and then we heated up two cans of meatloaf and ate.

"Do you think there are still chickens somewhere?" I asked.

"No, probably not."

"Or cows? Wouldn't it be great if we could catch one? We could have milk every day and make butter and cheese. Chickens would be great too. I'd love to eat some eggs again."

"They're domestic animals. They don't exist in the wild anymore, so I doubt they could survive on their own, which means no more chicken eggs or cow's milk. But other animals lay eggs. We'll just have to keep an eye out for them. And you can also drink goat's milk, but good luck catching a wild goat."

"That's too bad."

"Yeah."

We finished our meal and then I pulled out my peanut butter again. After I had some I offered half a spoon full to Troy.

"If I refuse, will you kiss me again?" he asked, grinning.

"I might."

"Then no fucking way I'm eating this."

I giggled, got up and sat down beside him. I leaned in and we kissed for a couple of seconds. When we parted Troy looked really happy, he had this glow in his eyes and he was beaming at me. My cheeks felt warm all of a sudden and I smiled back at him sheepishly.

"What if I still don't wanna eat it?" he asked.

"Troy!" I said sharply and glared at him jokingly. He laughed a little, took the spoon and licked it clean.

"Let's go to bed, I'm about to pass out," he said

"Yeah, I'm beat too."

We got ready and went to bed. He insisted on sleeping on the outside, in case of an attack, but I didn't mind. I cuddled myself against him and he laid his arm over me. It was really cosy and comfortable.

"This is nice," I said contentedly.

"Yeah, there just could be a little more room to the ceiling. It'll be hard to fuck you doggy-style in here."

"What? You will never do me doggy style, ever," I said disgustedly.

"Why not?"

"It's degrading."

"How is it degrading?"

"Because I'm not a dog you can just mount."

"So how do you wanna get fucked then?"

"I don't want to get 'f-ed' at all, if anything we'll make love, but I don't think we'll ever do that either."

"Why wouldn't we?"

"Would you let me make love to you first?"

"Fuck no."

"There you go."

"Come on, it would be unnatural, I mean, you're clearly the girl."

I propped myself up on my elbow.

"I'm not 'the girl', you jerk," I said indignantly.

"Of course you are."

"No, I'm a guy."

"I'm not saying you ain't, but when we'll become a couple one of us has to be the girl and it sure as shit can't be me, that would be ridiculous."

"Neither of us has to be 'the girl', so never call me that again, ok?"

"Fine, Jeez, you're so sensitive."

"You're sensitive too when it comes to making love, aren't you?"

"You're not serious about that, are you? You're just trying to test me or something, right?"

"No, I want you to experience it first, so you'll know how careful you'll have to be and how easily it can hurt."

"Don't you trust me?"

"I do, but it's like when you cut my nails. I know you didn't want to hurt me, but you just had never done it before. But when you realized how easily you could cut too deep you started to be very careful."

"I swear I'll be extremely careful when I fu...make love to you, alright?"

"So will I when I do it to you first."

"No fucking way. Jesus."

"Well, then anal sex is off the table."

"Why do you have to make such a fuss about this?"

"Anal sex is a very big deal to me and I'm really scared to do it. It's such an intimate act and it can be terribly painful. And it's not like we can just Google how to do it right, so there's a lot that could go wrong, you know? I'm not asking you to try it first to test or to punish you, but because it would help to ease my fears. And if you can't make that sacrifice then it's unfair to ask the same of me."

He hesitated for a second, and then spoke. "I guess you're right. I'm sorry."

"It's ok."

"So, I'm not saying I'd ever let you do that to me, but just theoretically, how would that work? Would you wanna pound me for hours in every position imaginable till you really get a feel for it or what do you have in mind?"

"No, of course not, I'd do it the same way I'd expect you to do it to me, slow, careful and tender, you know?"

"And it would be only the one time?"

"I don't know, maybe if I'd really enjoy it I'd want to do it again."

"Jesus... I mean... I see. But since you don't even let me slip you my tongue yet I'm guessing that's not something I have to worry about any time soon, right?"

"No, I mean, we're not even together yet. And if we do become a couple it'll still take a long time before we have sex."

"What do you mean by 'if' we become a couple?"

"I'm not convinced yet that it could work out between us. We're very different. So let's just wait and see what happens, ok?"

"I guess."

"I'm not trying to frustrate you, I'm just scared, you know?"

"I know and I'll try my best not to be impatient and to be supportive," he said sincerely.

"Thank you."

I gave him a quick kiss on the mouth and cuddled myself back against him.

"Good night," I said and yawned.

"Night."

It had already gotten dark, so I closed my eyes. After a while I suddenly felt him smell my hair, which made me grin, because I thought it was really sweet. I fell asleep soon after.

When I woke up in the morning, I was lying on my side and Troy was spooning me from behind. I turned around and clung to him.

"Morning," he said.

"Good morning. How long have you been up?"

"A while and guess what, I didn't grind my dick against your ass, not even once. That should score me some points, right?"

I giggled.

"Maybe a few."

"How do I score more?"

"By being sweet mostly and maybe by not cursing so much or at all."

"Alright... Hey, will you have peanut butter for breakfast again? Cause I'll need a lot of freaking convincing to eat some too."

"You could just eat it without coaxing a kiss out of me, you know? That would be an example of being sweet."

"Would that score me enough points for a kiss?"

I giggled again and rolled my eyes jokingly.

"You're really missing the point."

"I'm just kidding, I'll eat whatever the f...rick you want, no kissing expected."

"That's nice of you."

"Does it make you wanna kiss me by any chance?"

"Troy!"

"Hey, it's your fault I'm like this, not mine."

"Oh really?"

"Yeah, you're making me crazy. Before you came along I was a normal guy, minding my own business, but now all I'm thinking about all day is what you'll taste like when I finally get to kiss you for real."

"So, our kisses weren't 'real' to you? Maybe we should stop then."

"No," he said, sighing heavily. I leaned forward and kissed him for a couple of seconds.

"What was that for?" he asked.

"No reason."

"That's a good reason," he said and we both smiled. "Let's get up. We have things to do."

"Like what?"

"We have to break some wood, then we could go rabbit hunting and in the afternoon we should fortify the RV, so we won't have to worry about freaks getting in too easily."

"Ok."

We got up, had breakfast and then spent maybe an hour breaking furniture in the house. When we had enough wood we wheeled it to the RV and then went hunting.

CHAPTER 12

It was a beautiful day outside. There was barely any wind, so it wasn't too cold. The sun was shining brightly. A thin, fresh layer of snow on the ground was glistening in the light. It was peacefully quiet. After walking for a while I took Troy's hand in mine. He raised his eyebrows and looked at me in surprise.

"Does that mean we're together now?" he asked.

"No, I just wanted to know how it feels."

"But you want to be with me, right?"

"Maybe, I don't know."

"What's the problem? I mean, what's holding you back?"

"I have to be sure first that I want to be with you for the right reasons and not just because I have no other options. And also, I don't know how much commitment I can expect from you, which worries me. I know we said we'd stay together for the foreseeable future, but what if we do meet other survivors and there are girls among them? Can you guarantee me that you won't leave me for one?"

"I guess I can't. I mean, someone has to repopulate the earth, so I'd have to at least fuck them and then help raise my children. For the greater good, you know?"

"How noble of you," I said sarcastically and then continued, disappointed. "But that's exactly what I'm talking about. I don't want to be just a substitute and to be pushed aside as soon as the real thing comes along. I want a partner, for good, so I have at least one constant in my life."

"Don't you think you're reaching a little too high? In this world you have to be grateful for every little thing that is given to you. And we don't even know if we would work as a couple or how we'll feel about each other ten years from now. And so what if we wouldn't stay together forever? Even if we could make each other happy for only a couple of days or weeks it still would've been worth it, at least in my opinion."

"You're probably right, I just have this romantic idea of sharing my whole life with someone, growing old together, stuff like that, you know? But I guess that's stupid."

"It's not stupid, it's just not realistic."

"I know."

"But now it makes sense why it takes you so long to decide if you wanna be with me. It's not an easy decision when you wanna commit this fully and we've known each other for what now, a week?"

"Exactly and it'll be even harder now that I know how you feel."

"Hey, that's not fair. Do you want me to make you a bunch of empty promises? I don't even know if I can take your dick in my mouth without gagging yet."

"That's lovely," I said, rolling my eyes.

"Come on, you know what I mean."

"Yeah, and I'm sorry, but your attitude towards commitment is definitely a problem for me."

"Alright, is there anything else about me you don't like, that I could work on?"

"I'm a little worried about your temper, but aside from that I can't really complain, you've already changed so much since we met, it's quite remarkable."

"Well, I had a good reason to and it wasn't that hard, cause survival is all about adapting to any circumstances as quickly as possible and as I said, I'm a survival-machine. Also, I won't lose my shit again. You have my word on that."

"What makes you so sure?"

"Because it's different now. I've learned to trust you and to let my guard down and to accept that I'm at your mercy."

"That's good."

"I've also figured out how to handle you correctly, physically I mean. I just pretend that you're a talking raw egg made out of sugar and act accordingly."

"That's kind of insulting."

"When I kiss you, am I too rough?"

"No, it's perfect."

"See? It works. But I could be less careful if you want."

"No no, I guess there are worse things than being compared with a raw egg made out of sugar."

"There you go... How does it feel by the way?"

"How does what feel?"

"This," he said and held up our hands.

"It's nice."

We both grinned.

We walked around without talking for maybe ten minutes.

"I'm a little cold," I said.

"You can go back if you want."

"No, I have to protect you in case monsters show up."

I felt kind of silly saying that, but after Troy saving my life on several occasions it was the least I could do for him.

"I think I can handle myself, besides, we're fenced in, remember?"

"Still, I don't want to risk it."

The worst thing I could imagine at that point was losing Troy. And if he'd got killed and I hadn't been there to help him I never would've recovered from that.

"Why don't we spread out, so we can cover more ground? That way we'll be done faster."

"Ok."

We separated and for the next two hours or so searched the whole property, but without any luck, so we decided to return to the RV. I started a fire in the wood burner and soon it was nice and warm. I heated up two cans of soup and we ate.

"After we've fortified the RV, there's nothing else left to do, is there?" I said while we were eating. "Are we going to stay here or do you want to leave?"

"I don't know, the house is uninhabitable. The RV is great of course, but we can park it anywhere and it's really warm in California. We could drive along the coast and look for a new place, go swimming in the ocean and sleep on the roof, under the stairs, every night."

"That sounds nice."

"Let's rest for a few more days and then we'll talk about it again, alright?"

"Ok."

We finished our meal, had some peanut butter and then went to work. We had found a roll of chain-link fence by the barn, so we cut it up into smaller pieces and screwed two layers of them over all the windows. It was pretty difficult without a power drill. We had to punch out the holes for the screws with a hammer and we had to use a blanket to muffle the noise. We also built a new lock for the door, making it almost impossible to get in, even with a crowbar. When we were done I had a couple of blisters on the inside of my hand, but I didn't care, it made me feel like I could be useful after all.

At the end of the day we decided to reward ourselves with another warm bath and an elaborate meal. When I was lying in bed that night, in Troy's arms, I felt really content and grateful for how things had turned out. We had plenty of supplies, a great place to live and most importantly each other. There wasn't much more I could've asked for. I closed my eyes and fell asleep quickly.

We had left the barn doors open, to air out all the smoke, so I was woken by the sunrise. The sky was mostly purple and some orange shone through, something I hadn't seen before. I turned around, but Troy was still sleeping, so I gently kissed him on the mouth. He opened his eyes and grinned at me.

"Hey, did you just kiss me?" he asked.

"Yeah, I wanted to show you the sunrise."

"Gorgeous," he said softly.

"You didn't even look."

"I know," he answered and winked at me. I smiled and felt myself blushing.

"Oh, you. Now look outside."

He did.

"Yeah, nice."

"How about we stay in bed all morning?"

"I thought we could break more wood."

"No, we have enough wood and besides, I need some rest, look at this," I said and showed him my hand. He took it, blew on it and then kissed all the blisters.

"There, all better."

"Aww, that's so sweet."

"I'll do it myself then."

"No, you're staying right here, with me," I said, laying my head on his chest and my arm over his stomach. It felt so warm and snug that I closed my eyes for a moment to fully enjoy it.

"Fine, but we can't just stay in bed all morning."

"Why not?"

"I don't know, I was taught respectable people don't stay in bed longer than its dark outside, unless they're sick. Only bums and trailer trash do that."

"Well, an RV counts as a trailer and we don't have a job or any money, so we basically are trailer trash."

"Shit, you're right," he replied, laughing a little.

"Let's go back to sleep, ok?" I said and stroked his stomach.

"I could try, but I really feel like getting up."

"You have my permission to smell my hair from time to time. That should distract you for a while." I smiled.

He frowned.

"I don't wanna smell your hair." He protested.

"Sure you do. It's ok, I think it's sweet."

"But it's not true."

"Whatever you say. Hey, is there smoke coming out from under the blanket? Your pants must be on fire."

"Cody! I'm not lying!" he was clearly the one pouting now, but it was cute. I lifted my head and smiled at him.

"If you admit it you'll get another kiss." He opened his mouth, but hesitated and I laughed. "It's really nothing to be embarrassed about," I said.

"I don't even know why I wanna do it."

"Because you're attracted to me and my hair is loaded with pheromones, so if you smell it, it's like you're snorting heroin or something."

"Yeah, that's a good comparison. You're like a drug. I get more and more addicted to you and even though I know it's wrong, I can't stop."

"Excuse me?"

"You know what I mean."

"No, I don't. Are you saying loving me is wrong?"

"Of course it is."

"Why?"

"A man loving another man, it's against nature."

"No, it's not, there's homosexuality in nature."

"Yeah, but it's still wrong, cause those animals can't procreate."

"Not every animal has to procreate, that would lead to overpopulation. Homosexuality prevents that, which means it has a purpose."

"I haven't thought about it like that before."

"See? Also, if I'm an angel, God created me, and he's infallible, but I'm gay, so homosexuality can't be wrong, right?"

"I guess. But I don't care either way, I just want my fix."

I grinned.

"As I said, feel free to smell my hair whenever you want... Unless I haven't washed it in more than two days, then it's gross," I said and laid my head back in his chest.

"Hey, what about my kiss?"

"Oh, right, I forgot."

I lifted my head, leaned in and we kissed for a couple of seconds.

"Alright, now you can sleep," he said and we both grinned.

I laid down my head and closed my eyes again. After a minute or so I felt him smell my hair and I smiled to myself.

I dozed off, but maybe an hour later nature called. I looked up at Troy, but he had fallen asleep too, so I gave him a quick kiss. He immediately opened his eyes and smiled at me.

"You cheater, you were just pretending to be asleep so I would kiss you," I said.

"Hey, I just closed my eyes. It's not my fault you jumped to conclusions."

I looked at him suspiciously.

"So that wasn't intentional?"

"I didn't say that."

I giggled.

"Now I have to punish you."

"Oh yeah, how?"

"I don't know yet, maybe I'll pee in your soup a little."

"Your piss probably tastes like warm Fanta, so I don't care."

"Eww, that's just wrong. But speaking of warm Fanta, I need to use the bathroom."

"Alright, I'll open a can of breakfast for us in the meantime. Any requests?"

"Peaches would be nice."

"You're a peach," he said, grinning.

"What's that supposed to mean?" I asked, frowning, and he looked at me with a surprised expression. I knew I wasn't masculine, especially not compared to Troy, but that's exactly why it bothered me so much when he didn't see me as a real man. It made me feel inadequate, like I was worth less than him.

"I don't know. That you're sweet?"

"You usually don't say that to a guy."

"What are you, the language-police or something?"

"And what are you, an illiterate or something?"

He lifted his right hand, raised his middle finger and held it directly in front of my face.

"Bite me," he said and I tried to bite into his finger, but he quickly stuck it so deep into my mouth that it made me gag.

"What he heck was that?!" I asked indignantly.

"Didn't you like the taste of my finger?" he replied, laughing.

"Open your mouth, right now!"

"No thanks."

"Do it or I won't speak to you for two days."

"Oh really?" I just glared at him. He reluctantly opened his mouth and I stuck my finger in till he gagged. "Jesus, if someone were watching us they'd think we're insane," he said and I giggled.

"Well, one of us is."

"I think someone needs to get the shit tickled out of him."

"You know, wounded like that I could probably kick your butt now, so you better watch it."

"You couldn't kick my ass if I were tied to a tree. I can spit harder than you can punch."

"You're a jerk," I said and tried to climb over him, but he held on to me.

"Come on, I was only teasing you."

"So you think I could take you?"

"Sure," he said, grinning.

"You're lying."

"Alright, look, it's like I'm the snake and you're the snake charmer. I'm quick and deadly and you wouldn't stand a chance against me. But you're the one in control. You can make me do whatever the fuck you want. So who do you think has the real power?"

"Me."

"That's right."

"I need to go."

"Are we good?"

"Of course."

He let go of me and I climbed out of bed, put on some clothes and hurried to the toilet. When I came back Troy handed me an opened can of peaches and disappeared too. He was gone for a while and I was just about to look for him when he came through the door. He sat down across from me and grinned.

"Are you ok? You're a little pale," I said.

"Yes, I'm fine."

His breath smelled really bad. I frowned.

"Did you throw up?"

"Yeah, the stench got to me."

I held my hand against his forehead.

"You don't seem to have a fever."

"I'm not sick, don't worry."

"Let's hope not or I'm getting sick too."

"You won't. Now, any peaches left?"

"Sure, here."

I handed him the can and when he drank the juice out of it I giggled.

"What's funny?" he asked.

"Does it taste like Fanta?"

He frowned and held the can to his nose. I laughed.

"You're just fucking with me, right?"

"You will never know."

"Here, drink some."

"Eww... I mean, no thanks," I said and smiled innocently. He looked unsurely at the can and I laughed again.

"This is not funny."

"Yes it is and I thought you wouldn't care."

"I don't," he said and downed the juice in one go. "Mmh, delicious," he mumbled and I laughed.

"That's gross, but now we're even."

"Jesus, you actually did piss in it, didn't you?"

"Of course not, but I made you think I did."

"You little shit, now you need to get punished."

"No, come on, let's just go back to being nice to each other, ok? Please?"

"Fine... What do you wanna do today?"

"There's a CD-player in the front and I've found a couple CD's in the glove compartment. It's only classical and folksy stuff, but still, its music. We could go back to bed and listen to it for a while."

"That'll drain the battery pretty fast and it's probably really old, so we don't know how long it'll last."

"Only for half an hour or so, that won't drain it completely. Please?"

"Alright, why not."

"Great," I said, smiling.

"I'll start a fire while you choose a CD."

"Ok."

I went through the CD's and finally picked Beethoven's 'Moonlight Sonata', because it was the only thing I knew. I put it in the player and turned down the volume a little. Troy was still busy with the fire, so I climbed into bed and waited for him. When he joined me I covered us up and cuddled myself against him. Soon it was really warm and cozy and Troy was gently stroking my back. It felt good to listen to music again and the piece was beautiful and very moving.

I started to think about my life and how grateful I was for finding Troy and all the things we had. I suddenly realized that I was genuinely happy and was a little overwhelmed by the feeling. A tear ran down my face and I sniffled softly.

"Hey, what's wrong?" Troy asked concerned. I lifted my head and looked at him. He frowned when he saw the tears in my eyes. I could see how worried he was and how much he cared. I leaned forward and kissed him long and passionately. I felt bad for leading him on again, but I couldn't help myself, I just wanted to show him my appreciation somehow. When we parted he frowned again.

"What was that for?... Not that I'm complaining," he said.

"Just for being sweet."

"But we're still not together, right?"

"No, I'm sorry."

"But we will be soon, right? I mean, you wouldn't kiss me all the time if you didn't want to be with me, would you?"

"I feel connected to you, yes, but I don't want you to break my heart, so I can't and probably won't let that happen. Do you think you could settle for just being really close friends, who occasionally give each other a kiss?"

"No," he said, smiling.

"Then why are you smiling? I thought you wanted to be with me."

"I'm just happy, that's all," he said softly.

"Ok... How do you like the music?"

"It's kind of cool and pretty soothing."

"I like it too. When we're on the road we could listen to it every night."

"That would be nice... Are you still sad?"

"I wasn't sad."

"But you were crying."

"They were happy tears."

"I see."

He kissed my forehead and we both smiled. I laid my head back on his chest and we continued to listen to the music. When it ended I got up, turned off the CD-player and tried to start the engine. Thankfully it did start.

"Now what?" Troy asked.

"We could read the sequel to 'The Hitchhiker's Guide to the Galaxy'."

"Sure."

"It's almost time for lunch, should we eat first?"

"Why don't we skip lunch and break more wood later, to really work up an appetite and then have an elaborate dinner tonight?"

"Ok, sounds good."

I got back in bed with the book and read to Troy for a couple of hours. We had a lot of fun and laughed constantly.

Later in the afternoon we went to the house, gathered all the rest of the useable furniture and broke it into smaller pieces. Soon it started to get dark.

"Can you finish up in here? I'll get dinner ready," Troy said.

"Sure."

He left and since I wasn't thrilled about being by myself for too long, especially in a dark house that reeked of death, I worked as fast as I could. When I was finally done about twenty minutes later I filled the wheelbarrow and headed to the RV. The curtains to the driver's cabin were closed and the inside was brightly lit. The light was flickering though. It suddenly occurred to me that the RV might be on fire and that Troy could be in trouble, so I panicked, quickly ran to the door and opened it.

CHAPTER 13

The curtains to the driver's cabin were closed and the inside was brightly lit. The light was flickering and it suddenly occurred to me that the RV might be on fire and that Troy could be in trouble.

I panicked, quickly ran to the door and opened it. I sighed in relief when I realized that he had just set up a few candles. But then I entered and saw that the whole room was filled with them. Troy was standing next to the table, smiling at me.

"What's all this?" I asked.

"I need to ask you something."

"What?"

He went down on one knee and pulled out a golden ring.

"Cody, I know this is crazy, but I've said it before, you make me crazy. You want commitment? You got it. I hereby swear to stay with you for the rest of my life, no matter what. I also swear that I will always protect and cherish you. Now, it may sound silly since we can't 'officially' get married, but we could just cut out the middle man and pledge our loyalty to each other in front of God. So, do you wanna be with me, for good?"

This gesture meant so much to me, it was exactly what I wanted and needed to hear. It couldn't have been an easy decision for him, but it only showed how much he loved me. And I knew he was sincere, he always was. I felt so overwhelmed with happiness that I couldn't hold back my tears.

"I do," I said shakily.

"So do I."

He took my hand and slipped on the ring, then he handed me a second one and I put it on his finger. He got up and we kissed passionately. When we parted we smiled at each other and I stroked his face.

"Let's eat," he said.

"Yeah, I'm starving, but we should blow out some of these candles first."

"Don't you like them? In movies they always have lots of candles when they propose."

"No, I love this, it's very romantic, but they're kind of a fire hazard and you can see the RV from a mile away."

"You're right. You blow them out and I'll set the table."

"Ok."

About five minutes later there were only two candles left, on the table, and dinner was ready. Troy had made roast beef with rice and peas and he had even opened our last bottle of wine.

"To us," he said.

"To us," I repeated. I touched his glass with mine and we both took a sip.

"Hey, why don't you sit over here, where I can do stuff to you more easily?" he asked, grinning.

"What kind of stuff?"

"You'll see."

I got up and sat down beside him. He laid his arm over my shoulders and kissed the side of my face. We both smiled and then started to eat. Troy had trouble getting the peas on his fork with only one hand, which made me giggle.

"Why don't you just take your arm off my shoulders?" I asked.

"Does it bother you?"

"No, not at all, but you could use your second hand to eat."

"But then I wouldn't touch you anymore... You're making no sense. Are you drunk already?"

I giggled.

"That's really sweet."

"And I'm not even doing it to score points, since I can now kiss you whenever I want."

"That's not true."

"What do you mean?"

"You can't kiss me whenever you want, only when I allow it."

"Well, that goes without saying."

"I hope so."

After we had finished our meal I pulled out my peanut butter and we fed it to each other.

"Wait, you threw up earlier, so you might be sick and we shouldn't use the same spoon or even kiss for that matter," I said.

"I'm not sick. I puked when I got the rings."

"Oh my god!" I said, shocked, and frowned deeply. I quickly held the ring to my nose, but it only smelled of cleaning products.

"Where did you think I got them?" he asked.

"I hadn't thought about it, but it probably brings bad luck taking wedding rings off a corpse."

"No, it's perfect, they obviously stayed together till the end and now we can continue their tradition."

"You want one of us to die and then kill the other? Those aren't great prospects."

"If it'll happen when we're old and after we had a long, happy life together then I won't mind going out like that. And if we'll still love each other too much to stab the other in the head when he dies then there's no way around it. It's kind of romantic if you think about it, like a really fucked up version of 'Romeo and Juliet'."

"I guess."

"Do you like the ring at all? I know it's nothing special, but it's gold and it fits, that's something, right?" He looked at me with wide eyes, obviously hoping for my approval.

"As far as I'm concerned it only matters what they mean to us, not what they look like, so I like them very much." I said.

We both smiled.

"That's good." He smiled.

"Do you want to go to bed now?" I asked.

"And make out?" He was again wide-eyed, and cute as ever.

"Yeah, sure." I said, and I could tell he was overcome with pride as I took his hand in mine, and kissed him softly on his cheek.

We both quickly used the toilet, brushed our teeth, undressed and lay down. I was on my back and Troy was on his side, leaning over me. It felt so exciting, because we were a couple now and would be really intimate for the first time. We started to kiss and after a couple of seconds he touched my lips with his tongue, so I opened my mouth and let him enter. Our tongues met and he was surprisingly restrained and gentle, which made me smile and I broke the kiss.

"What's the matter? Was I too rough? I tried to be really careful," he said, concerned.

"No, not at all, I just had to smile, because I never would've thought you'd be such a great kisser."

"It's easy, I just listen to my first instinct and then do the exact opposite."

I giggled and stroked his arm.

"Keep doing that. It's working."

"As you wish."

He leaned down and we started to kiss again. This time I entered his mouth and our tongues caressed each other. After making out for a while he suddenly reached into my underwear and took a hold of my penis. It startled me and I quickly grabbed his hand and pushed it away.

"What the heck is wrong with you?" I asked sharply.

"What? I was initiating the 'love making'."

"No, there won't be any love making, because I'm not in love with you yet. And you can't just touch my private parts without asking first."

"Why not? I'm your boyfriend now."

"That doesn't give you the right to do whatever you want with me."

"I was only trying to make you feel good."

"Well, it didn't make me feel good, it made me feel violated."

"Jesus, you're so fucking sensitive."

"And you're an insensitive jerk," I said indignantly and turned my back to him.

"Come on, I'm sorry, alright? It won't happen again, I swear. Please don't let this ruin this perfect day."

I turned to him again.

"Ok... I'm sorry too. I guess I overreacted a little. I just didn't expect you to do that and it startled me."

"It's fine and now I know better... Are you still in the mood to make out?"

"Not so much. Could you maybe just hold me instead? Please?"

"Of course."

I cuddled myself against him and he laid his arm around me.

"So I guess I'm back to scoring points, right?" he said.

"To get into my pants?" I asked, frowning.

"No, your heart."

"Oh, yeah, you could say that."

"By the way, you have really nice 'private parts'."

"Troy!" I said, pretending to be indignant, and playfully slapped his stomach. The truth was that I did feel kind of flattered, but I was still embarrassed and probably even blushed.

"Sorry."

"It's ok... Hey, let's go to sleep, I'm really tired, probably from the wine."

"Sure, good night," he said and kissed my head.

"Good night."

I fell asleep pretty fast.

***

The next morning I was once again woken by a spectacular sunrise. I was on my side and Troy was spooning me. He held on to me with his right arm, so I laid my hand over his and smiled.

"Good morning," he said, then leaned down and kissed my cheek.

"Good morning."

"Hey, could I ask you something without you getting mad at me?"

"That depends on the question."

"So couldn't I ask you this 'off the record' and when it's inappropriate we'll forget all about it?"

"Ok, shoot."

"Can I touch your ass? Above your clothes of course and I won't squeeze it too hard or pinch it or anything."

"I don't know."

"Please?"

"Fine, but this'll be an exception, ok?"

"Yeah, great."

He slowly let his hand slide down my butt, cupped it and then started to gently massage it. It felt surprisingly erotic and I really enjoyed it, especially when he probed the area between my cheeks, but I felt so embarrassed about it that I stopped him.

"That's enough," I said and he immediately pulled his hand away.

"Was that so bad?"

"How would you feel if I'd grope your butt?"

"So you didn't like it?"

"Not really," I lied. The truth was, I wanted him to touch me again pretty badly actually, and more than that even, I felt a deep desire for us to pleasure each other, but I was afraid to go too far too fast. This relationship had to last, so I didn't want to rush into anything and jeopardize it by letting it become too physical before we had built a strong emotional foundation first. I had read about couples whos emphasis lay on sex right from the beginning and when the passion started to fade after a while they realized that they had never learned how to connect emotionally and how to relate to each other, which created a rift between them and they eventually broke up. I was really worried that that could happen to us.

"I'm sorry, I won't do it again," he said disappointedly and a wave of guilt washed over me.

"No, you can, just give me some time, ok?"

"Yeah, of course."

I turned around and kissed him lustfully. When we parted he looked a little flushed, which made me smile.

"Wow, if you still kiss me like that you couldn't have minded me groping you that much after all," he said.

"No, I just forgive very quickly."

"I'll say. By the way, your ass is the motherfucking bomb. Who knew."

"What do you mean by 'who knew'?" I asked, frowning.

"Who knew a guy's ass could be such a turn on. I can't wait to touch it without the clothes. I could spend hours studying it. Hopefully someday soon you'll let me."

Me too, I thought.

"We'll see," I said and kissed him again. He pushed me on my back and started to stroke my chest and stomach.

"Doesn't that hurt? Lying on your side and using your arm like that?" I asked.

"Yeah, it does, but it's worth it," he said, grinning, and I giggled.

"We could change positions, you know?"

"Maybe later."

We continued to make out and after a couple of minutes he suddenly slipped his hand under my shirt. I quickly grabbed it.

"Troy, I thought we've been over this," I said.

"You said I can't touch your 'private parts' and I'm not."

"Well, you can't do that either."

"Why the hell not?"

"Because I don't want you to."

"So only first base then? Fucking fourth graders go further than that."

"Are you saying kissing me isn't enough for you?"

He lay down on his back and touched his forehead.

"No, of course not," he sighed. I turned away from him and started to cry.

"Oh shit, no, I'm so sorry, I'll behave from now on and I won't pressure you anymore, I swear. You can take as much time as you need, I don't care. Please stop crying," he said nervously. I turned around and clung to him. He took me in his arms and stroked my back.

"I'm really sorry I'm like this," I said sadly.

"No, you're perfect."

"Please don't say stuff like that or you'll really get me going."

"Sorry."

"The truth is, when you touched me, I liked it, maybe even a little too much and I don't trust myself. I don't want to do anything with you. I mean, I do, but I'm really scared to... You know?"

"What are you scared of?"

"That our relationship will only revolve around sex and become shallow and emotionally disconnected. And also that you'll stop being sweet, because you won't have to score any more points."

"Wow, I didn't expect that..." he said, frowning, but looked at me sympathetically. "First of all, I want you to be happy, that's my priority, and if me being sweet to you makes you happy then I'll always be sweet, alright? And second of all, after what we've been through in only one week now I'd say our relationship is already deeper than it could've been after a couple of years before the apocalypse. And we need each other, depend on each other and we're all we have in the world. I don't know about you, but I feel so intensely connected to you it's like you're a part of me. Sex would only be the cherry on top and it's not like we'll be able do it every day. We probably won't have enough water to wash ourselves very often, so we'll be too dirty to do anything most of the time."

I giggled.

"I feel kind of stupid now."

"Don't, I'm just really fucking smart."

I laughed.

"And modest apparently."

"No, not so much."

"Thanks," I said sincerely.

"For what?"

"Saying the right things."

"Sure."

"But I still want to wait. Is it ok if we'll stay at second base for a while?"

"Of course, but you mean first, right?"

"No, I mean second," I said, grinning.

"Really? That's awesome."

"I know you want more and I'm sorry, but waiting might be fun too. The anticipation could make it that much more exciting when we'll finally go further."

"We just have to survive long enough."

"That's true, but I feel so safe with you, so that's not something I'm really worried about. But does that mean you're not ok with waiting?"

"No, I absolutely am. It's even kind of a relief actually, I mean, I'm still a little nervous about putting your dick in my mouth."

"Yeah, me too, but we can do it with our hands first."

"I can't wait... I mean, I can wait."

I giggled.

"We should keep our eyes open for lube, you know? Just in case we'll need it someday," I said.

"Do we have to have lube?"

"Of course. You'll be thanking me, trust me."

"Oh, right, cause I'll have to go first. You know, you'll probably end up being the one pushing me to have sex, not the other way around."

"If you'll be patient and understanding with me I'll be patient and understanding with you, ok?"

"Deal."

"Could you maybe start a fire?"

"Sure, how about you prepare breakfast in the meantime."

"No, I'm not getting up and you have to come right back to bed too, ok?"

"Alright, I can do that."

"Do you want to?"

"There's not much else I want more."

"You mean there are things you'd prefer over cuddling with me?" I asked, grinning.

"Maybe cuddling with you naked," he said and winked at me.

"I see."

He kissed the top of my head and got up. I scooted over to the edge of the bed and watched him build a fire wearing only his underwear. When he was done he joined me again and took me in his arms. I closed my eyes and listened to the flames sizzling in the wood burner. Soon the room filled with warmth. Troy was holding me tightly and I could feel him breathe in and out. In that moment I felt truly happy and I never wanted it to end. I was completely relaxed and after a while I dozed off.

Chapter 14

When I opened my eyes again I looked up drowsily at Troy, who smiled at me and gave me a quick kiss on the mouth, which made me grin.

"I wish we could stay here forever," I said softly.

"In bed?"

"No...Well, yes, but I meant here on the farm."

"So you don't wanna go to California?"

"I don't know, it'll be dangerous and we have no idea what's waiting for us there."

"Our future is waiting for us there and the sooner we leave the sooner we can start our new life together. Also, we could start growing food early enough for it to be ready by the time we'll run out of supplies. And what if the freaks are already dead over there? Besides, I wouldn't mind not freezing my ass off every day."

"I guess you're right, we need to go. The journey will probably be tough, but we have to bite the bullet sooner or later, so let's just get it over with. And who knows? We might be even happier over there."

"So you're happy right now, with me?"

"Yes, I am."

We smiled and kissed each other.

"How about we leave tomorrow?" he asked.

"Ok, sure... So let's enjoy today as much as we can."

"I already do," he said, grinning, and I smiled.

"Oh, you."

"Not to kill the mood, but I have to take a piss."

"Me too. You go first, I'll open breakfast."

"Alright," he said. He gave me a kiss and climbed out of bed, got dressed and left.

He was back five minutes later.

"Are you hungry?" I asked.

"I could eat."

"Why don't we skip breakfast and eat it for dessert after dinner, to save peanut butter?"

"Sure... Hey, do you wanna make out some more?"

"Again? It's only been two hours, at the most."

"So?"

"Maybe it won't be as special anymore if we'll do it too much."

"I'm willing to risk that."

We both grinned.

"Ok, but I still have to pee."

"Well hurry up or I'll start without you."

"I'd like to see that."

"Really?"

"No... Well, maybe."

"Interesting."

"I'll be quick."

I took my toothbrush and went outside. I relieved myself, brushed my teeth and hurried back. Troy was already in bed, waiting for me, so I promptly joined him.

"How about we take our shirts off?" he asked.

"Ok," I said and we both took off our shirts. He leaned over me and started to stroke my chest and stomach. I closed my eyes and moaned softly. I felt him kiss my right nipple and then he moved up till our lips met. We made out for a while and he continued to touch me tenderly. I had never been this aroused in my whole life and I wanted to do more really badly, so I turned on my side, with my back to him.

"Press yourself against me," I said.

"Are you sure?" he asked.

"Please." I smiled.

I could feel his erection between my butt cheeks. I started to grind against him rhythmically and we kissed passionately. I couldn't stop myself any longer, so I took his hand and rubbed it up and down against my own erection. After a few minutes I felt the pressure rise and when it was released the pleasure that pulsated through my body was almost too much to bear and made me tremble. I moaned loudly and pressed my eyes shut. When I had recovered a minute later I started to move again and kissed Troy longingly. Suddenly he tensed up, moaned ecstatically and then his whole body collapsed.

"Holy shit, what the hell was that?" he said, a little out of breath.

"Did you like it?" I asked innocently and he laughed.

"Hell yes. I mean, Jesus, what has gotten into you?"

"I guess you make me crazy too."

"That really was crazy. How could that feel so incredible? We weren't even naked."

"We probably just both really needed that."

"Maybe. Do you think it'll get even better than this? Cause I can't imagine what that would look like."

"I bet it will, if we'll wait long enough."

"This is definitely worth the wait."

"Yeah... We should clean ourselves up."

"I'll get us a towel or something."

"Ok, thanks."

He got up and looked through the kitchen cabinets till he found a dish rag and gave it to me. I cleaned the inside of my underwear and handed it back to him. He took it and held it to his nose.

"Nooo, eww," I squealed and tried to grab it, but he was faster.

"That's mine now," he said, grinning.

"No, come on, that's gross."

"Not really and I wanna get used to it, so I won't gag when I blow you."

"Fine, then I want one too."

"Sure."

He took another rag, cleaned himself with it and then let me have it. When I sniffed it I wrinkled my nose and frowned a little. It didn't smell very good, kind of like my own, not horrible, but bad enough that I didn't want it in my mouth.

"What's the matter? Don't you like it?" he asked.

"I'll get used to it."

"But you're gay."

"So I have to automatically love sperm? That's offensive."

"Oh, I'm sorry, I didn't know that."

"It's ok."

"Do you want me to come back to bed?"

"Of course. Do you?"

"That bed is now my favorite place in the world, of all times."

We both smirked. He climbed up and I cuddled myself against him.

"When we're on the road we'll stop at night and sleep, won't we?" I asked.

"Yeah, I guess we could do that, the RV is pretty secure after all."

"Good."

"Hey, wouldn't it be cool if we'd meet a famous actor or singer in California? He or she could reenact movies or sing for us," he said.

"Yeah, who are your favorite actor and singer?"

"I'd say Denzel Washington and Corey Taylor."

"Who's Corey Taylor?"

"From 'Slipknot'?"

"Oh no, those maniacs with the masks?"

"Exactly, they're awesome. They were I mean."

"No, they were insane."

"Who do you like then?"

"Meryl Streep and Mariah Carey."

"Jesus," he said, laughing.

"What? They were both amazing."

"Yeah, but to pick those two as a guy is just really fucking gay... No offense."

"So? I am gay."

"Sure, to each his own I guess."

"At least none of them was mentally ill."

"Whatever."

"What if we'd find someone like Megan Fox? Wouldn't you be tempted to do something with her?" I asked.

"No, I'm yours now, remember? Besides, being with a guy has turned out to be pretty fucking awesome so far, so I wouldn't feel like I'm missing out by not fucking a hot woman."

"That's a good answer. I would've kicked you out of bed if you had said yes or maybe."

"Trust me, I'm pretty loyal."

"I'm glad to hear that."

"Wanna make out?"

"Ok, but no more than that and we should get dressed first."

"Sure, whatever you want."

We put our shirts back on and started to make out. After what felt like a long time I was getting hungry, so we decided to take a break to eat something. We heated up two cans of soup, sat down beside each other and Troy laid his arm over my shoulders again.

"Hey, I have an idea. We should take a bath," he said.

"Yeah, it'll probably be our last chance to do that for a while."

"I meant... together."

"Oh. I don't know."

"No funny business, only holding each other."

"But we'd be naked."

"We've seen each other naked before."

"Yeah, but we'd be... 'excited'."

"It's up to you, it was only a suggestion."

"Ok, but we have to control ourselves, we've already gone too far today."

"Sure, no problem."

"Fine."

We both ate quickly and then filled the tub together. It seemed to take forever for the water to heat up. When it was finally warm enough we both undressed and looked at each other. I felt really exposed and nervous and the fact that Troy's penis was a lot bigger than mine didn't help. He must've sensed my discomfort, because he came very close, till we were almost touching, and kissed me tenderly.

"You're amazing," he said softly and I felt myself blushing.

"You're not too bad either."

"Shall we?" he asked and I nodded.

He went in first and sat down. I joined him, leaned back against him and he laid his arms around me. I slowly started to relax and closed my eyes.

"I love you, you know?" he whispered in my ear and I almost felt my eyes water up.

I couldn't believe how much he had changed and how much he meant to me already. It felt so intimate and sensual lying there pressed against him. He was tenderly stroking my stomach and chest and was constantly kissing my neck, which gave me goose bumps every time, the good kind. I would've stayed with him in that tub all day, but after about half an hour the water wasn't warm enough anymore.

"We should get out," I said.

"We still have to wash ourselves. How about we wash each other?"

I should've said no, but I really wanted him to touch me.

"Ok."

"Great, I'll do you first."

He picked up the shampoo from the floor and after he had massaged it in I dipped the back of my head into the water and rinsed out my hair.

"Get up," he said and we both got up. He took the shower gel and started to lather me, but he did it very slowly. He cleaned my left hand first, worked his way up my arm, over my shoulders, to my other arm. Next he went down my chest and my back at the same time and then turned me a little, so he could get to my butt more easily. He gently and thoroughly cleaned both cheeks and then slowly slid down in between with one finger. When he reached my anus he massaged it for a few seconds, which made me tremble with excitement. He moved on and let his hand slide all the way to the other side. He turned me again, cupped my testicles and then took a hold of my erection and slid up and down on it a couple of times. I suddenly felt weak in the knees and leaned against him for support. He must've realized what he was doing to me, because he let go, kneeled down and started to lather my legs. Lastly he did my feet, which tickled. I quickly rinsed myself off in the water and then it was my turn.

I did it the same way he had, but when I came to his butt I didn't want to risk making him uncomfortable, so I left out the area between his cheeks. His penis was next. I wanted to touch it, but I hesitated and wondered if it would hurt a lot having it inside me. Considering the size I was glad I didn't have to find out any time soon.

"You don't have to touch it if you don't want to," he said.

"No," I answered and quickly took it in my hand, which made him grin. It felt different than my own, heavier and a little softer somehow. I only slid up and down on it once, because I didn't want to tease him too much. I finished washing him, we got out of the tub, and dried ourselves off. When we were dressed he pulled me close to him and kissed me.

"Thanks," he said.

"My pleasure," I answered and we both grinned.

We did our laundry together and then went back to the RV. While Troy was hanging up our wet clothes I brought in the wood that was still in the wheelbarrow. When we were both done and the fire was burning again we sat down beside each other at the table.

"What do you wanna do now?" he asked.

"We could read."

"Sure."

We climbed into bed and read for a while. Later in the afternoon, when it was starting to get dark, we made dinner and ate. For dessert we had peaches.

"What a day," I said.

"Yeah and it's not over yet. We can make out some more before we go to sleep, right?"

"I guess, but no funny business, ok?"

"Alright, fair enough."

"And tomorrow we'll leave in the morning?"

"That's the plan."

"I'm scared. The stakes are higher now, because we have a lot more to lose."

"And to gain. Besides, God is on our side, so nothing bad will happen, you'll see."

"I hope you're right."

"Come on, let's go to bed and I'll take your mind off things."

We both smirked.

"Ok."

We undressed and climbed into bed. Troy leaned over me and we started to make out. After a while he found his way under my shirt and stroked me tenderly. Soon I was on the verge of losing control again.

"We have to stop," I said huskily.

"We do?"

"Yeah or I won't be able to hold myself back any longer."

"You don't have to, you know?"

"No, but I want to, I'm still scared, I'm sorry."

"It's alright, I understand."

"Thank you."

"Sure."

"It's kind of funny that I'm the one having trouble controlling himself, not the other way around, isn't it?"

"Yeah, that surprised me too."

"I didn't think we'd have such incredible chemistry. And you're really attractive, that doesn't hurt either."

It felt a little embarrassing talking about my sexual feelings. It was just all very new to me, so I was still insecure about it.

"You're pretty hot yourself, but you're very sensitive and fragile, I think that's what's holding me back."

"I'd be offended, but it's probably a good thing that you see me that way."

"Yeah."

"We should get some sleep. Tomorrow's going to be a long day."

"Alright, good night." he said, gave me a kiss and lay down on his back.

"Good night."

I clung to him and he took me in his arms. I had a hard time falling asleep, because I couldn't stop thinking about the journey ahead of us and what the future might bring. I prayed silently to God, thanking him for all we had and pleading for his good grace and protection.

In the morning I was woken by Troy gently kissing me. It was still dark outside. I opened my eyes and we smiled at each other.

"It's time to go," he said softly.

"I know," I answered worriedly and frowned a little.

"Don't be afraid. It'll be fine. In a couple of days we'll be in California and we'll be happier than ever."

"Let's hope so."

He leaned down and kissed me long and tenderly. I stroked his hair and we smiled at each other again.

"Come on," he said. We got up, dressed and had something to eat.

After checking if everything was secure Troy sat down behind the wheel and I in the passenger seat. I took the travel atlas out of the glove compartment and he started the RV. Soon we came to the gate and I jumped out to open it. After driving through we decided to close it again, in case someone else were to find the farm someday. We headed west and eventually found our way back to the main road. I could see the sun rise in the side-view mirror. Its soft light bathed everything in the most warm and beautiful reddish colors. I marveled at this spectacle, but then I suddenly noticed two monsters walking across a snow-covered meadow, which snapped me back to reality. They were moving very slowly, like they were tired. One of them was missing an arm and their clothes were soaked in blood that hadn't completely dried yet, which lead me to believe that they had recently killed someone. I felt the anxiety building up in me and I looked over to Troy. He smiled at me reassuringly and it really calmed me down. That's when I knew, as long as I had him by my side, everything would be ok.

End of Book 1

MORE IS COMING.

SPECIAL BONUS CHAPTER

FROM BOOK 2 ON THE NEXT PAGE

CONNER ADDICOTT

AN APOCALYPSE ROMANCE NOVEL

ROAD TO CALIFORNIA